CW00867604

Bedtime Stories For Kids:

Meditation Sleep Stories for Children & Toddlers (Ages 2-6, 3-5)

For Deep Sleep, Developing Mindfulness, Relaxation, Anxiety & Bonding with Parents

By Jessica Jacobs

Table of Contents

Spick, Span & Mayhem

Once upon a time, there were three elves. The first elf had long, shiny blonde hair, small pointed ears and eyes as blue as the sky. His name was Spick. The second elf had tight, springy curls on her head, clever hands that could play almost any instrument and skin the colour of chestnuts. Her name was Spick. The third elf had wild orange hair, long, spindly arms and legs and skin the colour of paper. His name was Mayhem.

The three elves lived together in a beautiful cottage in the middle of Evergreen Forest. Evergreen Forest is a magical place where it is always summer time. The trees stay green, plants grow all year round and the elves could grow food, collect water and play outside any time they felt like it. They ate berries growing on bushes, apples from the trees and potatoes they grew in the ground. Their games of hide and seek could last for hours as they climbed from tree to tree, hiding in the undergrowth and disguising themselves in the plants and bushes. It was a happy, sunny place to live.

They all enjoyed playing together, but Mayhem very rarely won any of their games. Spick could arrange the branches of the tree to hide himself completely, until he was almost invisible. Span could creep as quietly as a tiny mouse through the forest and no one could hear her coming. Mayhem, however, wasn't so lucky. No matter how he tried to step lightly and gently, his feet crashed through the forest and everyone could hear him coming for miles around. When he tried to whisper *hello* to a bird or caterpillar or rabbit, his voice boomed towards the sky, shaking the leaves in the trees.

Spick and Span tried their best to always be patient, but sometimes Mayhem could be very disruptive. He could trip and fall into a berry bush and squash all the fruit. Spick and Span would have to stop gathering berries to help Mayhem wash his sticky clothes. At night, while Spick and Span quietly slept, sometimes Mayhem would snore loud and long, like a horn blowing. Other times, he would breathe quietly but huge gusts of wind would billow around the room, opening up all the cupboards, turning over the fruit bowl and causing the windows to rattle!

Mayhem liked living with Spick and Span but sometimes he felt sad. On days when he burnt the food for dinner, or accidentally flooded the kitchen or tripped over the neat wood pile and scattered the logs across the floor, Spick and Span would sigh. They would say,

"Mayhem, be careful! Mayhem, please try to be more gentle! Oh, Mayhem, don't get in the way!"

Sometimes Mayhem wished he could be more like Spick, with his ability to clean the cottage from top to bottom in a matter of minutes. Or more like Span, who could wash the dishes, harvest the vegetables and chop wood before playing her beautiful music, neatly stacked wood around her and all the dishes tidied neatly away.

One day, Spick said,
"Today is a day I must visit the market in the village! We need some soap and some salt and some new socks."

Span nodded and began to gather her things into a bag: her purse, fresh fruit and water for the trip and a little pipe to play while they walked. Mayhem looked up from the book he'd been reading. He opened his mouth but Span shook her head and looked at him sadly,

"I'm sorry, Mayhem. You can't come today. We really need these things and we can't risk upsetting the people at the market. Don't you remember, you knocked over all the-"

"I remember!" Mayhem interrupted, "I'll be fine here."

Spick and Span left after breakfast. Mayhem felt sad. He tried to read his book, but he couldn't concentrate. He washed the dishes, but accidentally broke one of the bowls when he dropped it. He practiced climbing the biggest apple tree, but he rattled the branches and caused dozens of apples to thunder down around his head. He tried to paint a picture of the cottage, but somehow spilled paint all over his clean trousers. He set down his painting things, curled up on a soft, thick patch of grass in front of the cottage, and fell asleep in the sunshine.

Mayhem was woken up a few hours later by a very small, very rough tongue licking his nose. He opened his eyes to see a beautiful, tiny kitten watching him. The kitten leapt into Mayhem's wild tangle of hair, digging her paws into his orange curls. Mayhem sat up, cradling the kitten with one hand until she was nestled into his shoulder. Spick and Span were setting down heavy bags of shopping. They looked very weary but both of them were smiling brightly.

"The farmer gave her to us," said Span, "He had too many to take care of them all and thought she might like to live in the woods."

The kitten leapt from Mayhem's shoulder and began chasing light little scraps of leaves as they were blown by the gentle breeze.

"I think he was right!" said Mayhem, What's her name?

"We're not sure yet… we thought you might like to choose."

Mayhem smiled broadly before furrowing his brow, "It might take a little while…"

Spick and Span sighed at one another. Mayhem usually rushed into things, but when he took his time to make a decision, he *really* took his time.

"It's okay, take as long as you like. We'll call her Kitten, for now."

Kitten rolled onto her back and stretched all four of her tiny legs towards the sky, before settling down and closing her eyes to go to sleep.

For the first week Kitten lived in the cottage with Spick, Span and Mayhem, everything was good. Kitten played amongst the plants and flowers while the elves dug up potatoes, she watched them playing hide and seek together and she fell asleep on top of Mayhem's bed at night, while listening to Span playing her music and Spick singing along.

One day, Mayhem was throwing out yesterday's bread for birds to eat, while Spick and Span were cooking dinner. Span neatly chopped garden vegetables while Spick prepared the herbs. Spick carried out the vegetable scraps to put into the compost heap, and called to Mayhem,
"Is Kitten with you?"

Mayhem dropped the loaf he'd been tearing up and ran over to Spick, his arms and legs flailingly wildly and his hair sticking up from his head. He looked very worried,

"I thought she was playing inside?"

Spick tried to tell Mayhem not to worry, but he was very upset. He knew that if Kitten was lost, she'd be very difficult to find. She was very small and made hardly any noise. She was still too young to meow properly!

Spick called Span to come into the garden and the three elves sat on the grass in a thinking circle. Usually a thinking circle was used to come up with a way to mend a leaking roof or to make up a new song. Today, in the thinking circle, the elves thought about where Kitten could possibly be.

"She could be in the wood pile," said Spick.

"Or in one of the cupboards!" said Span.

"What if she's wandered far away from the cottage and can't find her way back home to us?" Mayhem said, quietly.

Spick and Span held Mayhem's hands gently, and tried to reassure him.

Span said, "Okay, we just need to make a plan. We'll split up, one of us will walk down the path, one of us will look amongst the trees and one of us will look in the house."

Spick nodded, before pointing at the sky, "It's getting dark, quickly. We'll need torches, and maybe-"

"NO!" Mayhem roared. A flock of starlings were startled from a nearby tree. Mayhem leapt to his feet and shouted, "Kitten will be frightened and if we don't find her right now, something terrible might happen! What if she's lost or stolen? What if she's hurt?"

Before Spick or Span could say another word, Mayhem ran into the vegetable patch, blowing out his breath in a huge gust that made all the leafy vegetables flutter in the breeze. He puffed again and the leaves lay down flat; some of the carrots were even pulled out of the ground from the force of Mayhem's breath. Kitten was not hiding in the vegetable patch.

Mayhem ran to the wood pile and with a gentle push of his hand, the neat pile collapsed, wood rolling in all directions. Kitten was not hiding in the wood pile.

Spick and Span realised Mayhem's plan. He was tearing apart the neat, tidy garden to find Kitten as quickly as possible. They soon began shouting encouragement,
"Look in the house, Mayhem!" Mayhem ran into the cottage and all of the cupboard doors flew open. Mops, brooms, plates, biscuits, tea cups, tea towels and spoons flew across the room. Kitten was not hiding in any of the cupboards.

7

Finally, Mayhem blew a gust of breath and the curtains billowed and the clothes leapt out of the drawers and the wardrobe and the blankets on the bed landed in a heap on the floor of the bedroom. Two bright little eyes peered out from beneath Spick's bed. Mayhem wriggled under the bed to rescue Kitten. She'd found a ball of wool and had become so tangled up while she was playing, she couldn't get out from under the bed! For the first time, Kitten opened her mouth and made a tiny, little *miaow!* Mayhem knew he was saying thank you.

After all of the excitement, everyone was hungry. They ate dinner sitting outside the cottage and watched the sun setting over the forest. Mayhem looked into the cottage, "Oh dear, he said. What a mess!" Spick and Span both smiled.

"Don't worry," they both said, "We can all tidy up tomorrow. Let's go to sleep now."

And the three elves and Kitten made a fort out of the blankets and pillows on the floor of their cottage and collapsed in an exhausted heap. As they were drifting off to sleep, Mayhem whispered, "I think I've discovered your name, Mischief!" and the kitten purred happily in reply.

Away with the Fairies

John loved to play in the garden. He could spend hours practising skipping, trying to climb the wall between his garden and the one next door and playing make believe games with his sister, Anna. But Anna had started going to school a few weeks ago, and John found the afternoons long and boring without her. Sometimes his Mum would come outside and play for a while, but she had lots of important things to do and couldn't play with him all the time. For the first time in his life, John started to feel a bit lonely, sometimes.

One day just after lunchtime, John ventured all the way down to the very bottom of the garden. He wasn't really supposed to go down that far- in the winter time it could be very boggy and squelchy down there, and Mum said he might slip and fall. In the summertime, brambles grew along thorny vines. Mum and Dad helped Anna and John pick them, but they weren't supposed to go there themselves. The bramble bushes had been there for a long time and the thorns were thick and sharp. Thick enough and sharp enough to give Anna or John a very bad cut.

John looked up at the kitchen window, which faced the garden. He couldn't see Mum. She might be doing the ironing or writing e-mails on her computer.

John just wanted to see if there were any good sticks, at the bottom of the garden. There were trees down there and he needed a good stick to play at knights and dragons. A sword-sized stick. He told himself he would go down very carefully, just for a quick look, and would come back straight away. He wouldn't go all the way down. He was just going to look.

As John walked cautiously down the slope of grass towards the bottom of the garden, he noticed it smelt different. There was a dark, rotten kind of smell and some nicer ones too, smells of flowers and plants. The flowers here looked smaller and brighter. John noticed there were some tiny mushrooms, too. He knew not to touch any of them, in case they were poisonous. He couldn't see any sticks, and it looked like it was going to start raining. There were dark grey clouds high above his head. John was almost ready to rush back to the house when he saw a perfect circle of little white flowers and mushrooms. He wondered if he could fit both of his feet in the little circle. He dared himself to try, before he went home. But John only managed to put one of his feet inside the circle before something extraordinary happened to him.

John landed with a soft *whump* on his back, on top of a patch of something soft. He was very surprised to open his eyes and find himself looking at a clear, blue sky. Soft white clouds floated and the sun shone brightly. It didn't look like it was going to rain at all. How could the grey clouds have disappeared so quickly?

John reached around to feel the back of his jumper. It was dry. He felt the soft thing he had landed on. It wasn't the soggy grass at the bottom of the garden. It was silky and smooth, like a soft pillow. John stood up and realised he was standing on something big and floppy and pink. He peered over the edge of the pink mound and saw a big, yellow circle. What was this place? Before John could ask himself any more questions, an enormous helicopter flew over him. He ducked down onto the soft pink thing as his hair and clothes billowed wildly around him. The helicopter landed on the yellow thing. *It must be a helicopter pad*, thought John.

But when he lifted his head, the helicopter was not a helicopter at all. John was looking at an enormous, fuzzy, stripy bee! At first he felt very frightened, but then the bee said,

"Hello. Are you alright? You look a bit lost."

John jumped back up to his feet. He wasn't sure what to say- he'd never met a bee before. And this one was abnormally enormous.

"Hello, he began, I... I like your wings. They're lovely. Do you know where I am? I am a bit lost, actually. Well, in fact, I think I might be very lost."

The bee settled himself into the flower and gestured around himself with his front two legs.

"Don't worry. This happens sometimes. This," the bee spread out his little black arms, "is Fairyland. You must have stepped in a fairy ring or blown a dandelion clock thirteen times. Something like that."

"Fairyland?" said John. He looked all around himself, but saw no fairies. Just a huge bee and the strange thing he was standing on.

"Well. Where you are standing right now is a flower. An echinacea flower to be completely exact… You're fairy sized, at the moment. S'what happens, when you land here. If you were your normal size you'd squash us all to death!"

"Oh. Oh, I see. I didn't know that bees were so clever."

The bee gave a very dramatic sigh and rolled all five of his eyes.

"Yes. I hear that a lot from most of you who tumble down here, no idea what's going on. What is so surprising about an intelligent bee? Do we look stupid?"

John tried to apologise but the bee was already flying away, making his helicopter droning sound. He thought he was going to be left in the middle of a flower petal, with no idea where he really was or how he was going to get home. Luckily, after a swoop and a loop around the flower, the bee hovered beside John.

"Come on then, hop on! We haven't all got the time to be standing around in echinacea petals and daydreaming!"

At first John felt frightened, but the bee's back was soft and fluffy. He settled down into the black and yellow fur and held on tightly. John had ridden a horse, once, and tried to remember what he'd been taught. As the bee rose into the air, he realised that riding a bee was nothing like riding a horse. John took a big breath and focused on hanging on tightly.

The bee floated up and down gently as he flew. *Not like riding a horse*, thought John, *but a bit like riding a carousel at the fairground.* He took another big, deep breath and opened his eyes, which he'd had tightly shut since take off.

The ride was wonderful. They flew amongst tall, sharp-looking blades of grass and beautiful bright and scented flowers. John recognised some of the same smells from the bottom of the garden, some rotten and some sweet.

John laughed with joy as they ducked and dived in and out of the plants. The bee, clearly cheered up by John's enjoyment of his first ever bee-ride, called out, "Hold on!" before flying underneath and around a dandelion clock. The wisps of white, fluffy seeds scattered through the air. They were taller than John and the bee but light as air. John asked the bee,

"Is it magic?"

And the bee replied, "Flying? That's not magic, it's just the same as you walking. This, however, is magic…"

All of a sudden the bee rose above the heads of the flowers and the grass. John's eyes widened. There were buildings, steam and smoke, music and lights, chimneys and windows. It was a city! All around the base of an enormous wooden wall, stretching up into the sky. They landed beside this huge wall and John pointed,
"What is that?" He had never seen anything like it in his life.

The bee looked at him for a long moment, shaking out his coat where John had rumpled it, "It's a tree. Haven't you ever seen a tree before?"

John blushed. "Of course I have. Just… not from down here!"

"Hmm. I suppose," the bee shrugged and nodded.

As he spoke, a tall, thin man appeared from beneath one of the enormous roots of the great tree.

"Now," said the bee, "Burr, here, will look after you. I've got some pollinating to do this afternoon. It was nice to ride with you. I'll say hello if we ever meet, you know… on the other side!" And he was off.

John began to panic, realising for the first time since he'd landed on the soft pink petal just how unusual his situation was. He'd disappeared from the bottom of his garden, where he wasn't allowed to play, and turned up in a completely different world where he didn't know anyone or anything. He felt a hand on his shoulder, and he turned round with a shout of fear.

"It's alright," said Burr. He was taller than John with long, long hair decorated with lots of tiny flowers and stems. "I'll show you what to do, now."

John was too afraid to even run away, "Are… are you nice?"

Burr laughed, "*Most* fairies are nice! It's a bit like teachers… I bet almost all the teachers in your school are nice, right?"

"I'm not at school, yet," John answered, "But my big sister is and she says they are mostly nice. But one or two are quite horrible!"

"Exactly! Just like fairies. What's your name?"

"John."

"Okay John, let's get you to work!"

Burr walked off quickly, and John knew he was expected to follow him. He began to feel worried again. What did Burr mean by 'get to work'? Was he stuck here forever as a slave to the fairies? He felt as though he might begin to cry. Surely his Mum would have noticed he was gone by now? Oh, how was he going to get back home?

Burr turned a corner, and John found himself amongst hundreds of shiny, intricate spider webs. He gave a small cry of fear.

"Don't worry. We know not everyone likes spiders. Though they are really the most lovely company, I promise you. Anyway, there are none here now, just the lines. Come."

Burr led John to a huge barrel, made out of dry husks of pine cones. There was a lovely, flowery smell coming from the barrel.

"Okay, it's laundry day, so I think we'll have you on this for a while. Then you can go."

"Go? Home?" John smiled, breathing a huge sigh of relief.

"Didn't Mel explain to you?" It was Burr's turn to sigh, "That bee, honestly. He should have explained. When you fall into a fairy ring, we ask that you help us with some chores for a while before we take you back. A long time ago, fairies used to capture people who fell into a ring, but we don't do anything like that nowadays. It's a bit pointless, really."

John nodded, relieved that he was going to go home again.

For the next few hours, John and Burr worked hard together. John shook out wet clothes from the pine cone barrel, and handed them the Burr, who hung the clothes over the strong lines of spider web, to dry. The clothes were beautiful. Soft shimmering dresses, leggings with butterfly patterns dyed into them, coats and cloaks made of soft leaves and petals. They had been washed in water scented with flowers, and John daydreamed happily as he worked. Eventually, he reached into the barrel and felt its bottom; there were no clothes left.

"We're all done!" Burr said, "I can take you back now. That was fast- have you done this before?" John shook his head. He felt sad.

"Do I have to go back?"

"Ahh. You like it here? I'm sorry, but we can't keep you forever. Isn't there someone waiting for you?"

"Well, yes, Mum. And my sister will be home soon from school."

"I bet she'd like to hear about your day today. And you can ask her which teachers are nice and which are not so nice." Burr winked. "Tell you what. I'll give you something to take home. Don't tell anyone where you got it, though! You'll get me in trouble."
John cheered up a little bit. They were walking away from the bustle of the fairy city, towards a dark path. "What were you doing when you stepped into the fairy ring?" Burr held up a hand and they stopped walking.

"Looking... looking for a stick. A long, dry stick. To be a sword!" John felt a little embarrassed to tell Burr about the game he was playing, but Burr didn't make fun of him. Instead, he reached both hands behind his back and, half a second later, produced two long, pale wooden sticks. They were perfect- John saw the sticks but before his eyes they became swords, ships oars, walking staffs, sceptres, torches...

Burr bowed as he handed over both the sticks, "One for you, and one for your sister. Now, follow the path. I'll watch until you're gone."

John didn't know how to say thank you. He held up his hand, and Burr copied him. John had to jump up to reach, but he managed to give Burr a high-five. Burr laughed,

"I will remember that one! Go on now, John."

John walked up the dark, dark path. Soon he couldn't see his feet. Then he couldn't see the magic sticks. Then he couldn't see anything at all. And, in two blinks of his eyes, the sky reappeared about him.

"John! John!"

He sat up. Anna was at the very top of the garden. Rain had begun to lightly fall.

"Come one, what are you doing down there?! You're all wet! Get up here before Mum catches you!"

John looked down. He *was* all wet. And quite muddy, too. His shoes had slipped right through the little circle of flowers and mushrooms, breaking the ring. He gathered himself up to race to the house and tell Anna all about his afternoon. Before he went, he looked around for his sticks. He found them quickly and rested them beneath the hedge, to keep them safe and dry. They were not fairy sized anymore, but the perfect size for him and Anna to play with.

When John reached Anna she said, "What have you been doing?! Come inside and get dry. Hopefully the rain won't last too long and we can go out to play later. I've been stuck inside at school *all day!* What were you doing?"

"Hang on," John smiled, "I'll go and get changed and then I'll tell you. You won't believe what happened to me today…"

The Horses & the Bird

Once upon a time, two young horses were playing together in a lovely meadow. They were eating mouthfuls of sweet, juicy grass, racing one another and kicking their way through tall daisies, making the flowers shiver and shake. The grey horse was called Mercury and the black horse was called Nero. When Nero stopped to catch his breath after winning three races in a row, he heard a strange little sound.

It was a sound Nero had never heard anywhere before and so he swallowed his tasty mouthful of green grass and held his breath to listen. It almost sounded like a tiny child saying, "Oh, oh, oh!", or the noise acorns make as they fall from the tree. Then Nero spotted a tiny flutter of movement, deep in a bush at the end of the meadow. He lowered his head to investigate. His hot *whuff!* of breath startled the tiny bird hiding in the hedge.

Nero had never heard a bird making that kind of sound before. He wanted to ask the bird what he was doing, but then he realised. The tiny bird was crying! Nero used his softest and most polite voice, "Hello? Excuse me? I was just wondering, are… are you alright?" The bird looked up at Nero from inside the bush, big tears falling from his shiny black eyes.

When the bird didn't reply, Nero added, "I am Nero and it's nice to meet you."

The bird gave a wretched sob, before saying, "I am Hop. And I am so sad!"

"Sad?" Nero shook his mane, "Why would you feel sad? It's a beautiful day today!" He gave an excited *neigh!* hoping his enthusiasm for the sunshine might cheer up the sad little bird. But the bird wasn't ready to be cheered up.

"Yes, it is a nice day for a horse who can run and leap and trot across the grass as you can! I'll never ever know what it's like to be able to run, or jump high like you can. I can only… well, hop."

Nero was absolutely astounded, "But… but… you can *fly*!" He shook out his mane once again, "I may be able to run like the wind, but you can fly through the air! You can visit the sky! That is something I will never be able to do."

The bird had stopped crying. He was watching Nero, suspiciously, through just one of his beady black eyes. Then he said suddenly, "I can *what*?" Nero's laugh shook the branches of the bush, "You can fly. With your wings. Haven't you ever flown before? How old are you?" The bird clung onto his branch. It was still swaying from Nero's laughter. "I'm not sure. Not very, I don't think."

Nero scanned the sky. Soon, he spotted a flock of geese. He said, "Look, now, in the sky. You're only a little small bird, they're far away but much bigger than you. But you can do what they are doing right now. Little bird, you can fly." The horse suddenly had a thought, "Wait a minute, how did you get into the bush?"

"Well. I… climbed. Like the other birds." Nero took a long time to think about what the bird could mean. A pretty little brown field mouse darted out from beneath the bush, off to look for some lunch. "See! There's one now. I've seen her climbing too."

This time the horse gave a huge laugh, a laugh so loud that Mercury, who had been grazing at the other end of the meadow, came trotting over to see why her friend was talking to a bush and laughing. The bird was a little grumpy as Nero explained to Mercury, laughing all the while, that the bird thought he was a field mouse and had no idea he could fly. Mercury could see the bird was upset. She said seriously, "Well, how could he know for sure? There are no mirrors in the meadow. And I haven't seen any others like him for a few weeks."

"What are you going to do now then, silly bird?" Nero asked.

Mercury replied very quickly, "What are *we* going to do, you mean. You and I will help him learn to fly."

Nero wanted to argue that neither he nor Mercury knew how to fly or how to teach someone else to fly. But Mercury was a bossy horse, so Nero stayed quiet. He'd grown to like the bird, anyway.

The three of them spent an afternoon, the horses running and Hop stretching his wings over and over, practising. He tried taking off from the inside the hedge and from the ground and, eventually, from the top of Mercury's head. It took a long time to learn, but Hop was soon laughing, as happy as the horses were to be playing in the sun.

Eventually, Hop could fly. He could take off from anywhere he liked, he could choose the direction he wanted to fly and he could land without too much of a crash. Nero and Mercury watched him fly high, up over the tree-tops. Mercury gave a delighted *neigh*! It was Nero's turn to be serious.

"Why didn't Hop's family teach him, do you think?" Mercury pointed his nose to the trees, "There are no nests in these trees that I can see. Perhaps he doesn't have a family. He must have gotten lost somehow and ended up here on his own. Come, now, I'm very tired this evening. It's getting dark. Let's go to bed."

Nero was very quiet as he followed Mercury to their little shelter at the end of the meadow. He thought the little bird must be lonely, without a family. He had Mercury for company, and plenty of other horses came and went, cousins and aunties and sometimes his brother. Nero fell asleep dreaming of flying all alone.

In the morning, Nero and Mercury were both woken by a sound they'd never heard before. Nero opened one eye and saw Hop, perched on a fence post near their sleeping shelter. The bird was singing, a tune the horses had never heard before.

"Good morning!" Hop chirped, "It's time to wake up. Hear what I've learned already this morning! Let's find out what other new things we can learn today." Nero stretched happily, as Mercury told him quietly, "Now you don't have to worry anymore. I think that little bird has found a family."

The Rainbow Pixies

Once, in a land far, far away, there was a forest filled with tiny pixies. Thousands of pixies lived, quiet and unseen by any people, in the trees, beneath toadstools, by the stream and amongst the flowers. The pixies were all different colours. There were red pixies, yellow pixies, green pixies. Blue and purple and orange and pink.

The pixies did not, however, all live together. They lived in groups, according to their colours. The green pixies all lived in long grass or patches of soft moss or amongst the leaves in hedges or trees. The green pixies were usually very good at climbing or digging. The blue pixies lived by the pond or the stream and were all excellent swimmers. The purple pixies all lived in an enormous patch of purple heather. They had an excellent sense of smell, and could find food anywhere in the forest at any time of year. The orange pixies lived in huge piles of dried autumn leaves or on patches of orange clazy on the ground. These pixies made beautiful curtains and pots and pans.

The pixies would not live together, but they did meet once every twelve days in the market. There, the pixies traded one another for the things they could not make themselves. The blue pixies had water-plants to trade, which were bright green and extremely delicious. The orange pixies sold homewares, like pots and curtains and rugs. The purple pixies traded lovely foods from the forest floor; they were the only pixies who knew which mushrooms and plants were safe to eat and which were dangerous.

There was one last group of pixies, a group that were not just one colour. Some of them were a strange mixture of two colours, like turquoise or a very bright, pinkish purple colour. Some had hair and eyes which were a different colour from their body. Some had just one part of them that was the wrong colour: a yellow hand, a blue ear or a purple leg. These pixies lived in the places the other pixies didn't want. They were often cold, or damp, or hungry. The other pixies would talk politely to each other, but they ignored the multi-coloured pixies. This made them feel sad. The multi-coloured pixies had special talents, however, so they were allowed to trade in the market.

Martha, a blue pixie with very green eyes and pink hair, could summon bubbles from the stream and fashion them into floating carriers, so parents could take their small pixies with them before they could fly, without having to carry them. Some older pixies, whose wings were tired, used Martha's bubbles, too, for travelling in or for carrying heavy things. Lior was yellow with patches of blue on his arms and his face. He made special lamps. No one other than Lior knew how they were made, but it involved talking to a firefly, a shard of tree bark and the flower petals. The flower petals probably weren't necessary, but they made the lamps shine beautiful colours. Kai was a vibrant yellow-green colour; he could carve with no tools other than his own hands. He carved stones and pebbles into chairs, tables and shelves as well as beautiful sculptures.

One sunny day, Kai was sitting by the water, carving some pebbles into a family of smiling frogs. He was concentrating very hard on his work, as he hoped to trade the frog family at the market the next day. His pixie group wanted some new blankets, as the nights were getting colder. Nearby, a group of blue pixies were teaching their little ones how to swim.

Kai smiled as he worked. Sometimes he whistled or sang as he carved. Unfortunately, if the other pixies heard one of his group making noise, they often shouted at them to be quiet, or even chased them away. So, Kai kept quiet as he carved his frogs. That is, he *was* quiet until he looked up into the sky, trying to tell the time from the position of the sun. The smile disappeared from his face and he forgot all about his work.

He began jumping up and down on the spot, then hopping from foot to foot in excitement. He pointed up to the sky and shouted, "Look" Everyone, look" Look!" At first, the blue pixies in the stream scowled to have been interrupted by Kai, but soon they were pointing and shouting, too. Before long, lots and lots of other pixies began to emerge from their homes, green pixies from the trees, purple pixies from the lavender patch, orange pixies from piles of leaves. A very small, very wet blue pixie turned to Kai, "What does it mean?" she asked him. He was the one who saw it first.

In the sky was something the pixies had never seen before- a rainbow. Kai had no idea what to say, but hundreds and hundreds of pixies were now looking at him. He had no idea what it was! He'd never seen anything like it in his life.

They were all waiting quietly for his answer. "Well." He focused on the little pixie who'd asked him the question, "What do you think it means?" She looked thoughtful and Kai desperately tried to think of something. Luckily, the young pixie was less shy, "Well… it's all the colours together, isn't it?" she said. Kai nodded and looked around. Everyone had stopped staring at him. They were now whispering what the girl had said to him. The message was only heard by the pixies who were close to the edge of the stream, but soon they were whispering to each other, and passing the message further and further back, telling everyone who was watching. The whispering grew louder and louder, until pixies were shouting at one another, excited and alarmed by the colours splashed across the sky.

"Have I done something wrong?" the young pixie asked Kai. She looked very worried. "Not at all," he replied, "I think you might have done something very right." And then, because he wasn't sure what else to do, he picked up the smallest frog from the frog family, and gave it to the girl. The crowd became quiet as they watched and then, before anyone could say anything, before anyone moved a single muscle, the heavy, heavy rain began.

All of the pixies ran for shelter. Big raindrops could be dangerous to a pixie. A heavy drop could break an arm or leg, and lots of rain could even destroy their little houses. A green pixie suddenly raised himself up above the others, flying just above the crowd, "Listen! Take shelter in the trees, everyone! Our tree houses are the strongest structures in the forest!"

And that is exactly what everyone did. That day was forever known as 'the day the colours came together'. From that day on, pixies no longer segregated themselves into groups of colour. They shared food and shelter together and they taught one another their skills. The blue pixies taught swimming to anyone who wanted to learn. The pixies no longer decided what jobs to do based on their colours, but on what they were good at and enjoyed. Soon, there were families of all different coloured pixies. And now, if you were to visit that forest in that far away land, you wouldn't see a purple pixie, or an orange one or a red one. If you were lucky enough to spot one of the tiny pixies, they would be all the colours of the rainbow.

The Bravest Pirates

Once upon a time there were two very brave pirates, who also happened to be a dog and a cat. The dog had a brown patch over one eye. He called himself Captain Jack. The cat was a ginger tabby with a bend in her tail from one of their many dangerous adventures. She called herself Crooks.

One day, they were on their way home from a long and dangerous sea voyage, when they heard the wind carrying the sound of someone calling, "Help! Help!"

Captain Jack gave a bark in reply, then said to Crooks, "Come, we must divert from our route home and rescue the poor soul who's calling for our help!" Crooks narrowed her eyes, thinking. She asked her Captain, "Do pirates do rescue missions? I thought we just found treasure and kidnapped people for ransom and fought giant sea monsters?"

Captain Jack nodded. He was the Captain, but Crooks was an excellent first mate and she often had very good ideas. Finally, he decided, "Crooks, you may very well be right. But if you or I were calling for help, I hope someone would try to come find us."

"Very well," Crooks said a little grumpily, "I was just looking forward to getting to dry land, that's all..."

Captain Jack knew that a grumpy Crooks could be a big problem, so he said kindly, "Don't worry, we'll be ashore soon enough. I'm sorry to ask, but would you climb to the crow's nest and take a look around?"

Crooks scampered up the rigging to get a better view of their surroundings. She surprised the crow in his nest, who was nestled into her nest, hiding from the horrible weather.

"Is there going to be a storm?" the crow cawed. "I hope not," Crooks said as she looked far and wide. Then, she heard it again, "Help!" She could see how was calling for help and rushed down to the deck to tell her Captain.

"There's an island, Cap, not too far off. Sandy. Looks like a child calling. What should we do?"

Captain Jack didn't have to wonder what to do, "We sail to the rescue! Immediately! Especially for a child. I like children." Crooks wasn't quite sure if she agreed but they set off together anyway, the dog steering and the cat miaowing the directions. They found the island quickly; it seemed to be the only dry land for miles around.

"Oh. Hello," said the child, "I'm Luke. What are you two doing here? I'm all upset because… because… I lost something special in the sand here!" Captain Jack tried to comfort Luke, giving him a nuzzle deep into his neck and wagging his tail while Luke scratched his back. Crooks ignored them both and immediately began digging in the sand. When she was finished, there was a pile of sand beside her taller than her head, and she was standing patiently by the hole she'd made.

Jack woofed happily as Luke scurried over the ground. From deep inside the ground, he picked up a small black bag. "You've found them! Wow!" Luke was overjoyed. He tipped some of the contents from the bag into his hand to show the pirates. He held beautiful, tiny orbs, filled with swirling colours, shining even in the rain. Crooks desperately wanted to roll and chase one of the little spheres, but Luke clinked them into the bag and got up to leave.

He hurried off, looking for shelter from the bad weather. The rain was getting heavier and the wind was beginning to blow. From a far, far off distance, the pirates heard another sound. The call of home.

"Patch! Whiskers! Where are you both? Get in here now, it's dinner time. And it's raining!"

When Crooks and Captain Jack returned to land, they were tired and both could think only of a tasty meal and a long sleep on dry land. They ate dinner and fell asleep together curled up by the fire, dreaming of their next adventure together.

The Lost Rabbit

Mum and Dad and Sam woke up one Saturday morning to find beautiful sunshine streaming through all the windows of the house. Dad made slices of toast with marmalade while Mum went into Sam's bedroom to see if he was awake.

"Sam!" she said. Her voice was quite cross.

"Good morning, Mum. It looks like a lovely day outside," Sam yawned and stretched and sat up in his bed.

"Yes, it *is* a very lovely morning, isn't it? And where on Earth is Ronaldo?" Mum pointed to the other side of the room, at a big empty cage sitting on the floor. The cage had a water bottle attached to it and a cosy bed full of soft blankets inside. Sam knew he was in trouble.

"Mum, Ron is a *house rabbit*. He doesn't like having a hutch. He likes to have... house things. Like we do."

As Sam spoke, the bed sheets around his knees began to wriggle and squirm. A soft, cuddly brown rabbit leapt from the bed and onto the carpet. Ronaldo the rabbit hopped his way over to his cage to take a long morning drink from his water bottle. He didn't look at Mum.

"See? He knows when he's in trouble! He should be *inside* that cage at night time. He makes a mess, chewing things up! Now, come and get your breakfast, Dad is making us toast." Ronaldo looked up apologetically as Sam followed his Mum. Before he ate any of his toast, Sam washed some lettuce leaves and brought them to Ron for his breakfast.

Sam took a big bite of toast while his Dad poured everyone cups of tea.

"We're going to drive to the garden centre today, Sam."

Sam was delighted, "To get some things for Ron?"

Mum laughed and said, "You and that rabbit!" while Dad shook his head.

"Paint, Sam, for the garden shed. It's a lovely day, I thought we could paint it together."

Sam nodded. He would have to put Ron in his cage while he was out with Mum and Dad. Sam promised Ron he'd let him out once they were all back in the garden, so he could hop around the grass beside them. Ron twitched his nose in reply.

The garden centre was busy, because it was such a nice day.

"Oh dear," said Dad, "It looks like lots of other people may have decided to do some painting today, too!" Almost all of the paint was gone and only two colours were left on the shelf.

"Ah, I wanted brown paint, or maybe dark green. I bet it's all gone!"

Sam spun the huge tins of paint around on the shelf until he could read their colours.

"White… and purple!" Sam was excited, "My favourite colour!" Mum and Dad looked at each other with worried faces, then laughed, "It doesn't matter what colour the shed is, really!" said Dad. "Yes," agreed Mum, "And it is Sam's favourite, after all…"

It was very hot in the garden. Mum, Dad and Sam had all changed into old clothes, in case they were ruined with the purple paint. Sam was wearing old Batman pyjamas which were very short on his legs and decorated with several holes. He watched Mum stir the paint with a big, brown stick, while Dad wiped the shed to get rid of any cobwebs or dust, "They would make the paint go on lumpy!" he explained.

Mum gave a sudden shout of alarm, "Where did that rabbit come from! Sam? He's eating something!"

Dad dropped the cloth he was using and dived towards the patch of flowers, "Not my nasturtiums!" he cried out. He scooped up Ron in his arms. Ron definitely knew he was in trouble. He was hiding his face beneath his long ears.

"Sam. Fetch Ron's cage. He can come outside but he can't roam freely around while we're working here. He is such a nuisance!" Sam did as he was told but he felt bad for Ron, who settled down on the grass and looked longingly at the delicious plants and flowers in the garden through the bars of his cage.

Mum stood on a very tall ladder to paint the top of the shed. Dad stood up and painted the middle of the shed and Sam sat down on the paving stones to paint the bottom. Mum and Dad were very careful, but still paint flicked and dripped all over. Dad was lightly spattered with purple spots all over his face and arms. Sam was purple everywhere- his hair, his face, his old pyjamas. Mum didn't have very much paint on her at all. *She is doing the hardest job, though*, thought Sam.

Once the first coat of paint was on the shed, Mum said, "Right boys, time for more sunscreen, the sun is very hot today!" But dad looked at his paint splattered watch and said, "It's two o'clock! It's time for lunch. Come on, let's have a break." He helped Mum down from the ladder and she laughed at the site of Sam and Dad before stepping back to look at their work.

"Hmm…" she said, "It is *very purple…* isn't it?" Dad laughed and Sam cheered as they turned to go to the kitchen for a break. "You come, too," Sam told Ronaldo, lifting up a corner of the cage so he could hop out and follow them inside.

Lunch was tomato soup. Sam was smiling as he ate from his bowl. Tomato soup was one of his favourite foods. Mum and Dad were quiet, tired from the hard work and enjoying their lunch. When they were finished, Dad stood up to make a pot of tea and Mum went to the cupboard for some biscuits. She turned suddenly to Sam,

"Oh, we haven't left Ron out along in that heat, have we?! He'll be far too hot!"

"It's okay," Sam replied, "He followed us in." Sam ducked his head down to look underneath his chair, Ron's favourite spot during meal times. If they were having salad at the table, Sam often snuck Ron a few leaves. He had a book in his bedroom all about the different things rabbits like to eat, which he checked regularly.

But, Ron wasn't under Sam's chair this time. While Mum looked in the cupboard and Dad poured cups of tea, Sam slid down from his chair and crept off to find Ron. If he wasn't under the table, he was probably up to serious mischief. Once, he had chewed some of the big, soft cushions on the couch and made holes in them so the white, fluffy insides oozed out whenever someone sat against them. He'd also crashed into the coffee table and knocked over a vase of flowers. He could be quite a careless rabbit. Sam rushed through the house, worried Ron was going to get himself into some big trouble!

But Ron wasn't in any of his usual spots. Sam tried the living room first, but he wasn't underneath the couch, chewing the part of the rug hidden under the furniture. He wasn't in the big splash of sunlight on the floor in the hall, where he sometimes liked to doze off. He wasn't in the kitchen; Sam ducked right under the kitchen table to make sure. Mum and Dad were cleaning the dishes and singing along with a song on the radio. Sam crept off to the bathroom, then his room, and then Mum and Dad's room. But Ron wasn't anywhere to be seen!

Sam was beginning to look inside the cupboards in the kitchen when Mum and Dad realised he was behaving oddly,

"Sam, what are you doing? Are you alright? Had too much sun, perhaps?" Dad was holding a tea towel and smiling. Mum was not smiling, "I know what's going on. That rabbit. Where is he Sam, what are you cleaning up this time?"

"Um. I don't know. I haven't actually seen him since we came in for lunch." Sam could see his Mum and Dad were going all blurry in front of him. His eyes were filling up with tears. Mum knelt down beside him and she didn't look angry anymore,

"It's alright, Sam, he's probably still outside. Come on, let's go find him now."

Ron's cage in the garden was empty, as Sam had left it. The flowers didn't look any more nibbled than usual. Sam called for Ron but he didn't come out, "That *is* strange," agreed Mum, "He's not eating the plants. And he does usually come to you when you call for-" Mum stopped talking and gave an enormous *GASP.*

Sam ran over to her, afraid she'd found an injured Ron. But she was looking at the tin of paint. Somehow, lots of the purple paint had been splashed all around the tin. There were paving stones leading away from the garden, round to the side of Sam's house, and all the way to the spot where Mum parked her motorbike, at the front of the house. All along the paving stones were big splashes of purple paint.

Sam was worried Mum would be angry but she smiled, "It seems our mischievous friend has left us a trail to follow. Come on, let's go rescue Ronaldo!" Dad joined them in the garden, still holding his tea towel.

41

"Don't worry dad, the nasturtiums are safe!" Sam said.

"Hmm... that's good, but I'm not so sure about Ron. Let's catch him quickly and wash him. I don't think purple paint is all that good for rabbits."

Mum and Dad and Sam all followed the splotches of purple paint leading down the path. Beside some of the patches of paint, Sam could see little paw prints or scuffs where Ron's tail had landed. It took them less than five minutes to find the naughty rabbit. He was hiding underneath Mum's motorbike, his big floppy ears covering his eyes. Sam called his name, but he would not move. He was stuck underneath the motorbike. How would they get him out?

"He knows he's in trouble," said Sam. He hoped Mum and Dad wouldn't be too angry.

"Never mind that now," said Mum.

"Yes," Dad agreed, "We need to get him in the bath." Dad ran to the patch of nasturtiums, and picked the biggest, brightest flower. He held it out to Ron, who hopped over to Dad's outstretched hand, to take the tasty treat.

Dad quickly scooped Ron up in his arms, wrapping him tightly in the tea towel he was carrying. Ron squirmed and wriggled and struggled- he had given himself a big fright when he spilled the paint.

"It's alright, Ronaldo, we're just going to clean off the paint. And then you can have a nice carrot." Sam knew how to calm down his friend. At the mention of a carrot, Ron nestled into Dad's arms and let himself be carried into the house, up the stairs and into the bathroom. Mum turned on the shower head, making sure the water wasn't too hot. Dad lowered Ron into the bath, but he did not like being in the bath. He tried to hop out, smearing purple paint everywhere.

"Right," said Mum, "You're pretty dirty too, Sam, you've got tomato soup all over your face as well as that paint! In you get."

Sam climbed into the bath, still wearing his old batman pyjamas. Ron immediately leapt on Sam's knee, and looked at him imploringly.

"Sorry, Ronnie, we'll be as quick as we can."

Sam cuddled Ron and stroked his ears while Mum hosed them both with warm water. The water escaping down the plug hole was a vibrant purple. Sam gently cleaned Ron's fur.

"Silly, silly rabbit. You are always getting into trouble."

After their bath, Sam dried himself and got changed into clean clothes. When he went looking for Ron, he found the rabbit and Dad in his parents' bedroom.

Dad was drying Ron with a hairdryer, "So he doesn't catch a cold from being so wet!" Dad explained.
Ron *loved* the hair dryer. He wriggled happily in the hot air.

When Sam and Ron were both clean and dry, they sat in front of the TV, Sam with a packet of crisps and Ron with a carrot. Mum and Dad finished painting the shed while Sam and Ron watched cartoons cuddled up together on the couch. Ronaldo the rabbit was so glad that he'd been rescued that he was perfectly behaved for almost an entire day.

The Magic Snail

Anika was daydreaming as she walked home from school. Her school bag hung from the crook of one arm and she looked off into the distance as she thought about what her Gran might have made for her to eat that afternoon. She was so distracted, her eyes half-closed against the bright sun as she walked home, that she almost - *almost* - stepped on a bright, shiny thing right in the middle of the pavement.

Anika had never seen anything quite like it. It was iridescent, shimmering. From one angle, it looked greeny-blue, like the ocean. From another angle, it looked orangey-pink, like a pretty dress. If Anika moved her head quickly from side to side as she looked at the thing, it glistened with all the colours of a rainbow. It was a very mysterious, very strange thing. Anika dropped her bag and hunkered down on the pavement, for a better look.

It looked like a fantastic piece of jewellery. Anika looked around to see if there was anyone to ask, but there was no one around. She was just about to pick up the strange object and take it home to show her Gran, when she noticed a silvery trail of slime. The thing was a shell. Anika realised that, although it was a very unusual colour and resting in a very unusual place, the object was something she knew. It was a snail.

Anika decided that the snail must have been lost or confused to have stopped to rest right in the middle of the path. Someone could easily have stood on the snail- she herself very nearly had! Very, very gently, she picked the snail up and made her way to the side of the pavement, to hide him under a hedge to finish his nap in safety. The shell was surprisingly heavy, and large. It reminded Anika of picking up a heavy stone or a very juicy orange.

Anika was still wondering why this particular snail shell was so heavy when the next amazing thing happened to her. The snail popped his head out of his shell. He was big enough that she could clearly see his face. It was a very, very grumpy face. His voice was rather grumpy, too, when he asked, "Who are you and why are you picking me up without asking?"

Anika was so startled, she nearly dropped the snail! She knelt down and placed him just under the shelter of the hedge, away from the hot sun and any walking feet that might accidentally crush him. He did not notice her kindness,

"Leave me alone! I am tired, I don't have any energy left for talking to people! Or anyone for that matter!"

The snail's voice wasn't just grumpy. He was starting to sound angry.

"I'm really sorry to have woken you up," Anika said very politely, "But you were resting in a very silly place where you easily could have been squashed! I was only trying to help you. Please don't shout at me in that angry voice."

"So… so you don't know who I am?" the snail asked. He looked very surprised at Anika's outburst. She laughed at his question,

"No, I have no idea! I think you seem to be a very grumpy, very pretty snail. Also, quite a heavy one, too! But I don't have any friends who are snails, or insects at all for that matter, so no. I don't know exactly who you are!"

Anika lifted up her bag, ready to walk away from the rude snail. He called after her, and his voice sounded very different.

"I'm sorry!" he said, "I really am. It's just, I'm always being bothered by people, all the time, every day. I am so tired and it's so hot. I need a rest! I thought you were coming to ask me for wishes, but I see now you are just a kind girl!"

Anika stopped, and turned to the snail, "Wishes?" she asked. "Are you quite alright, snail. I've got to get home to my Gran or she will worry I've gotten lost. She has a lovely garden, lots of plants and flowers and grass. I could take you there. This hot pavement is no good for snails, really."

The snail looked as if he might cry.

"Really? You would take me to a nice garden?"

Anika smiled, "Of course! I would be very upset if someone did step on you. Even if you are horribly rude to people trying to help you, no one deserves to be squashed to death." She shuddered as she thought of it, and scooped him up before continuing her walk home from school.

"First if all, I am sorry for being rude. I explained to you. I'm a very busy snail and I'm in a bad mood because I'm tired. Secondly, I'm not an insect, I'm a mollusk. Thirdly... have you really never heard of me?"

Anika wondered if all snails were arrogant, or just the one she had happened to meet.

"No," she answered, "But I will listen as I walk, if you'd like to tell me."

The snail nestled cosily into the palm of Anika's hand, with a gentle *squelch*. Now he had stopped being angry, he did look quite sleepy.

"My name is Oden. I have lived for a very long time-thousands of years, in fact. I am of an ancient species of mollusk, a magical species. I believe my kind are now almost completely extinct, but we have always been very rare. For a magical mollusk like me to be born, a rainbow must form over a piece of volcanic rock three times between a full moon and a new moon. Very unusual."

"But… how have you lived so long without being stepped on if you sleep in the middle of the pavement?!"

Anika did not mean to sound cheeky, but Oden scowled at her question,

"I've *told* you. I'm really tired. Exhausted, in fact. I cannot remember ever feeling this exhausted. In fact, today may have been my time to die."

Anika didn't like thinking about dying, so she didn't look at Oden as she asked,

"Can you really grant wishes? Is that why you're a magical molsk?"

"Mollusk," Oden corrected. His voice was becoming more gentle, "And yes. I am able to grant four wishes to anyone who touches my shell."

Anika's eyes were round with wonder, "I thought that stuff was just in stories! And it's usually, three wishes, isn't it?"

"Well," Oden smiled up at Anika, "All stories have to come from *somewhere*, don't they? But they usually get some parts... mixed up. I don't know who first said it was three wishes... why would we grant an odd number of wishes? Four is much better."

Anika nodded quietly. *Four wishes,* she thought, *I wonder what I would wish for if I had four wishes?*

Oden interrupted her dreaming, "Are you thinking about what you'll wish for?" He sounded rather business-like, as though he'd asked this question thousands of times before.

"You mean... I really...?"

"Well, yes, of course! You've touched my shell. The three wishes are yours. Now, I will give you some advice, because you have been kind to me. People are usually very greedy and they waste their wishes quickly. Take some time to think."

Anika nodded again, this time very seriously. She felt very serious. It was a serious decision she had to make.

After a few more moments of Anika lost in her quiet thinking, Oden asked her, "Is it much farther? I'm drying out terribly. I could really do with some lovely damp soil."

"Just at the end of this street, don't worry." He did look quite dry, now. Anika hurried her footsteps as much as she could without jiggling Oden around too much. In her Gran's garden, she gently placed Oden under a leafy green plant with pretty violet-coloured flowers. He immediately looked much calmer. Almost peaceful. Anika left him enjoying the moist, cool soil and went into the house.

"Where have you been, girl?" he grandmother asked.

"Sorry, Gran, I was rescuing a snail that could have been trodden on!"

"Well, wash your hands quickly! You are kind, Anika. Come to the table once your hands are clean. I've made you a sandwich."

A very hungry Anika did as she was told, as fast as she could possibly manage. She took a huge bite of her sandwich before she noticed what her Gran had been doing when she came in. There were folded pieces of white paper all over the table, and brown and white envelopes. Gran had a very old calculator in her hand and a long, thin notebook. It was covered in writing. Anika couldn't read what was on any of the papers, though she did recognise her own surname: Khan. Her Gran looked really worried.

"Are you writing letters, Gran?" Anika asked, her mouth full of cheese and tomato sandwich.

Gran didn't look up from her calculator, replying, "Bills, honey, just lots of bills. There are always bills, never enough money..." Anika ate while she watched her grandmother work. She couldn't think of anything to say to make her Gran smile.

"Can I do my homework in the garden?" she asked once she was finished.

"Yes, of course, go on now." Her grandmother was still too busy to look up from the table.

Oden was very close to the place Anika had left him. He was awake now and eating leaves, slowly and happily. Anika sat down close to him, her school reading book in her lap.

"I think I know what I want to wish for," Anika whispered.

"Why are you whispering?" Oden asked.

"I don't want anyone to know there's a magic snail in the garden. They might steal you and then you will end up back on a pavement somewhere, ready to be squashed!"

Oden didn't want to think about being squashed at all. He knew Anika was probably right, so he kept his voice low, too.

"What are your wishes?"

"It's just one, at the moment. It's… well. It's I wish my Gran always had enough money and never had to worry about paying bills or buying food or getting me a new coat ever again!"

Oden gave Anika a strange look, "You know, most little girls would probably wish for lots of money, or a beautiful new coat or all the food they could ever eat. Your wish seems very sensible…"

"My Gran takes care of me every day," Anika replied, "And I want her to be happy."

"Very well," Oden smiled. It was very strange to see a snail smiling, but Anika thought it suited him better than his scowl. "Consider your wish granted."

"Just like that? No sparks or thunder or sparkles?"
"I am a snail, Anika. Don't be ridiculous."

Anika lay down on the grass and read her school book out loud to Oden. He helped her when she stumbled over a word and laughed when she read out using different voices.

When she was finished, Anika lay on the grass and watched the clouds drift slowly by.

"How long do I have to make my wishes?"

"Oh, well… I've never really been asked that before. Most people rush to make them all at once, more or less. I suppose… well, I suppose forever, really."

"Would you like to stay in this garden, Oden? And eat leaves and listen to me reading? If it's very cold in the winter, I could bring you inside the house."

"Hmm… I am not a pet," Oden said gently, "But I do like the sound of living somewhere I am very unlikely to be trampled to death!"

"Okay, then I wish-"

"No." Oden interrupted, "Don't use up a wish. I want to stay here. Thank you for inviting me."

Anika went to bed that night feeling very happy. Her Gran tucked her in. When Anika asked if she was worried about the bills, her Gran replied,

"Ah, Anika. I've been silly. There was one letter I missed, a very important one. We do not have to worry. Forget about the bills. All is taken care of."

Gran's smile was wider and brighter than Anika had seen in a long time and she could hear her singing in the kitchen. Anika drifted off to sleep thinking about Oden, the magical mollusk, happy he was safe in the garden and that she had three whole wishes, if she ever needed them.

Oden nestled underneath the leaves in the garden and heard Anika's Gran singing inside the house. It was the most beautiful sound he had ever heard. Oden looked around his new home and felt like singing, too. He drifted off to sleep thinking about Anika, the very kind girl who had saved him from being squashed and brought him to the nicest place he had ever lived. And she had three whole wishes left, if she ever needed them.

The World of Dragons

Lior slumped down in his chair at the dinner table, his chin almost touching his potatoes while his knife and fork hung loosely from his hands. He fell asleep and was immediately jolted awake by the clatter of his knife hitting the kitchen table.

"Hey," said his Mum, from far across the table. "What's the matter, Lior?"

Lior shrugged his shoulders. He couldn't be bothered to pick up his knife. He couldn't be bothered to finish eating his dinner. He slumped down further in his chair.

His sister, Hana, leaned over to him, and cupped a very cool hand around the back of Lior's neck. He almost jumped off his chair when she touched him.

"Fever." she said firmly. Hana was thirteen years old and very bossy. But Lior thought she was probably right.

"Drink some more water, brush your teeth and get into bed, little one." Lior hated when Hana called him *little one* but, once again, he thought that she was probably right. He argued with her anyway.

"If I go to bed so early, I will wake up in the middle of the night, a long time before school starts!"

"Ah," his Mum was shaking her head. "I don't think you'll be at school tomorrow. But we shall see. Off you go, now."

As much as Lior hated Hana making decisions and bossing him about, he felt too tired to protest any more, and did exactly as he was told. He sipped from his water glass and slipped from the table and into the bathroom. He used the toilet, swaying on his feet because he felt so tired! He washed his hands carefully and gently brushed his teeth. The inside of his mouth felt sore and tender. Lior was feeling more miserable by the second. It seemed to take him a long, long time to get into his pyjamas and onto his bed. He was feeling his cheeks and his forehead with his fingertips, trying to see how hot they felt, when his Mum came in, followed by Dad. Lior hadn't even heard him come home from work. Now that he thought about it, his ears felt a bit funny, too. Mum's voice sounded far away, so Lior told her so.

"I know, love," she said, "I think you are maybe coming down with something. Let me take your temperature." Lior obediently put the long, thin handle of the thermometer into his mouth. It always reminded him of the long, hard, brightly coloured sweets his grandad gave him when he visited. Lior knew the thermometer wouldn't taste of anything, but he still felt a little disappointed when he put it in his mouth. Mum took it from him and uncapped a bottle of medicine. That didn't taste nice, either.

"Right," said his Mum. "As Hana says, a little fever. Perhaps she'll become a doctor!"

"Or be in the police," Lior said, " Because she is very bossy."

Dad laughed, "Not too ill to be cheeky, I see! I think a good rest will help, Lior. I'm home from work all day tomorrow, so you and I can stay home together."

Lior sat up in his bed and tried to look well.

"Tomorrow Ms McEwan is reading us the last chapter of *The Land of the Dragons*. Please, please can I go to school? I've *got to find out what happens!*"

Mum and Dad were both shaking their heads gently. Hana came in from the hall, "You need lots of rest, Lior. Don't worry about the story tonight. You'll feel better soon."

Hana kissed the top of his head. Lior stuck his tongue out at Hana and she, Mum and Dad all wished him goodnight. They closed the door behind them and Lior could hear them turning on the television in the living room, all the way down the hall. As he tried to guess which programme they were watching, he fell into a very deep sleep.

When Lior opened his eyes, he was not in his bedroom. He was in a place of rolling green hills, huge violet skies and tall, ancient trees. He could hear the rush of water nearby, and turned around to see a river, full of bright, silvery fish leaping out of the current and landing back in the water with a *splash!* Lior knew exactly where he was:

"The Land of the Dragons!"

Everything was almost exactly as the book had described. The hills where dragons took off and landed, the brightly coloured sky where they flew and raced and whirled through the air together. Lior knew the dragons ate a kind of fruit that fell from those tall, ancient trees, a fruit which was the size of an apple but tasted of olives. They ate the silver fish from the fast-flowing river, too, and drank its water which was sweet and refreshing.

Lior felt a subtle shaking of the earth beneath his feet and heard a low boom, boom, boom sound, like the music Hana sometimes played in her bedroom. Walking along the edge of the river, towards Lior, was a dragon! This was a green dragon, with a bronzey-brown coloured belly. The dragon plodded along on four feet, which had enormously long claws on the end, which dragged a little on the ground and glinted in the sunlight as the dragon walked. The dragon had a huge body, as big as two houses, and a long neck, nearly as long as a giraffe, and a head the size of a car. The dragon's eyes were huge and shining, his teeth were long and pointed and very, very white. A huge tail swished lazily to and fro in the dragon's wake, much the same way that a cow's does, although this tail was a thousand times the size of a cow's.

The dragon bowed its head as it approached Lior, stopping a little way away before speaking.

"Hello. I am Athanas. I don't believe we've met one another before. Who are you, if you don't mind me asking?"

Athanas' words were polite but his voice was huge and booming, like his steps. Lior tried to sound brave as he replied,

"Hello Athanas. I'm Lior. I'm... well, I suppose I'm just visiting, really."

"Yes. And, excuse me once again but... what, exactly *are* you? You are like no kind of dragon I have seen before."

"Well. I'm not actually any kind of dragon. I'm a boy. Hang on... do you mean- are there different *kinds* of dragons? I thought dragons were all... well, dragons."

Athanas laughed while he shook his head. Lior still felt a bit frightened - Athanas was as tall as the tallest building Lior had ever seen, after all - but was feeling more relaxed by the minute.

"Of course there are. I, for example, am a Greek dragon: a *dracaenae*. If you would care to look," at this, Athanas swung his body around to one side, showing Lior his back and his enormous tail. It had a razor-sharp tip on the end, "I have no wings, as some dragons do," Lior noticed this for the first time and felt a bit silly he'd missed something so obvious. "Also, look, if you would, at my feet."

Lior realised that Athanas' feet did not have huge, shining claws but rather blade-like fins. They looked like wings for a fish, with webbing in between each separate fin-like toe. "And, I must ask you, are all boys like you? I didn't imagine they'd be so... well. Sweaty." Athanas looked at Lior apologetically.

"I suppose I am a bit... damp," Lior tried his best not to be offended. He had, after all, told Athanus he had thought all dragons were the same. "I've been feeling a bit poorly. I've got a fever. I'm very hot. And quite thirsty, actually."

Athanus smiled a sharp-toothed smile, "Excellent. Then we can make our way to the water... I'm far more at home there, you know. I was walking today to see where everyone else had got to... they must be down river. Shall we go hunting for them together, Lior?"

Athanus led Lior to the river, which he promised was safe to drink from. As Lior scooped water into his mouth and washed his hot face, the fat silver fish all hurried away quickly.

"Very clever, those fish," Athanus explained as he eased himself into the water beside Lior, "We used to eat them, a long time ago, but I never felt quite right about it. Of course, I do from time to time, if there's really nothing else, but I'm mostly vegetarian."

"A vegetarian dragon?" Lior's mouth hung open in utter disbelief. This time, Athanus did look a little offended,

"Yes. Most of us are, you know. We've got very high moral standards. Doesn't feel right to eat another living creature." Lior was realising things were a bit different from the book Ms McEwan was reading them. In the story, dragons ate horses and goats and sometimes people!

He told Athanus about the book while he climbed onto his scaly back. It was so wide he could sit comfortably, right in the little pocket between Athanus' shoulder blades, without having to worry about falling into the water.

"Hmmm..." Lior could feel Anathus' voice vibrating through his whole body as he swam, "It sounds like *some* things are really quite accurate... I mean, you did recognise this place from the descriptions in this book. But it missed quite a few things out."

"Exactly!" Lior replied. He had to talk very loudly over the sound of Athanus moving through the river, "I didn't know there were different kinds of dragons, or that they could talk, or swim, or that some don't have any wings, and I'd never think one would be a vegetarian!"

"It's not that unusual, really. Most things people know about dragons come from myths and legends. Second-hand stories, passed down and misremembered. The writer probably never visited Dragon Land, although it sounds like someone who *has* visited has told him about it… I've heard of this sort of thing before."

They travelled down the river under the bright sunshine. Athanus sang a quiet, beautiful song and Lior listened while he thought about all the stories he had ever heard, wondering how many had mistakes in them. He nodded off on Athanus' back and was woken up by a sound like a very loud and very badly-played trumpet. He was immediately wide awake. A shining, purple-black iridescent dragon nose was hovering just above his head. He looked up to see a huge silver eye staring right at him. The eye was bigger than Lior's head. He gave a shriek, and heard Athanus scold the other dragon,

"That's enough, Monty, let the poor boy alone. I'll come ashore and you can meet properly."

Athanus had been right, dragons could be very different from one another. Monty was not quite as huge as Athanus, but he was tall, standing on two hind legs. He had truly enormous, bat-like wings which the sunlight shone through. His wings were tipped with little claws right at the very top, which he seemed to use like hands, gesturing expansively as he introduced himself with a bow. He reminded Lior of a stage magician,

"My name is Montague and I am a *guivre*," he announced with obvious pride. Athanus rolled his eyes and bent his head low so only Lior could hear him, "Some dragons, as you may have noticed, can be very vain."

Lior tried not to laugh as Monty raised his chin and spread his wings to their full extent, as if posing for a photograph. It was difficult to be afraid of a dragon when they looked so silly.

"Ah," said Athanus, "Here comes Ciara."

A small, fast dragon flew through the sky. Ciara was a dragon with the speed and precision of an arrow. She landed gently beside Athanus and gave a smile to Lior. Her teeth were very long and very sharp. She was quite a bit smaller than the other two, but her voice was musical and calming, like the sound of a piano or a violin speaking aloud. Lior felt as though he would do anything she asked of him. He could feel that her magic was very powerful. He was feeling braver by the moment and wanted to introduce himself.

"Hi, Ciara. I'm Lior. I'm a boy. Are you the kind of dragon who flies the fastest?"

Ciara laughed and Monty huffed out his breath, clearly feeling outshone. Ciara answered Lior in her beautiful voice, "I suppose I am pretty fast when I fly." She tossed her head around in a big circle. She had stubby little horns and long ears flat against her head. Lior thought she was probably they most beautiful creature he'd ever seen, "But my real talent is this-"

Athanus said, "Careful, now," as Ciara padded over to the nearest tree. She turned her back on Lior, Athanus and Monty and raised her head.

Suddenly, there was an enormous noise, a whoooosh of air, like a very fast racing car or wind rattling through the house. Lior felt himself grow warmer as Ciara breathed a long, neat stream of fire into the tree. She was so careful, so precise, that just one branch was burned. It was burned so badly, however, that it fell from the tree and landed with a big thump on the ground. The fruit the branch had held bounced away in all directions,

"Is anyone hungry?" Ciara called over her shoulder, before setting off to help herself to something to eat. Athanus motioned with his head for Lior to go on. Monty followed them, muttering to himself that Ciara was a show off.

The fruits were only a little like the fruits in the story book. They were much bigger than apples, more like the size of mangoes, and they were all slightly different colours. Lior was quite hungry but he wasn't sure about eating a strange food. His Mum and Dad had always taught him not to eat fruit he'd found or bushes or trees. Athanus sensed Lior's hesitation,

"It's safe, boy, don't worry. The different colours are just different levels of ripeness. The dark red ones are the sweetest and the green ones are the least sweet. All are delicious. Help yourself, we have plenty to go around."

Lior trusted Athanus' wisdom and decided to taste some of the exotic fruit. He decided to start with the most savoury flavour. He chose a bright green one, and sunk his teeth into it. The fruit was very juicy and it did, like the book said, taste quite similar to olives. It was very. Very delicious and Lior ate the whole thing. Next, he tried a yellowish fruit. It tasted like a fresh salad, with a sweet lemony flavour, too. The orange fruit tasted like lentil soup. The last fruit Lior tasted was a very dark red, almost black, colour, That fruit tasted of chocolate and cherries and ice cream. It was the most delicious thing Lior had ever eaten.

After he was finished eating, Lior was very, very sticky. Athanus was too polite to mention that Lior was in a mess, but tactfully suggested everyone have a dip in the river to cool off. They played in the water, splashing one another and laughing. Athanus swam under the water, erupting to frighten his friends and soak them all in huge waves. Ciara shot warm arcs of water from her mouth, creating rainbow colour as the sun shone through the jets of water she sprayed. Monty whirled his wing through the river, creating a whirlpool that spun Lior around and around until he was dizzy.

They made their way back to the shade of the fruit trees to dry off. The day was really very hot. The three dragons lay peacefully on the ground and Lior curled up, too, in a little patch of clover. He sighed.

"We often have a nap around now, you now," Athanus said, and gave a little yawn. Ciara and Monty were lying close together, already drifting off to sleep.

"The others may be here, soon." Before Lior had time to wonder what Athanus could mean, the rustling of dry twigs snapping made him turn his head. A brightly shimmering red and gold dragon slithered through the trees towards them. The dragon was so bright Lior had to squint his eyes.

"Here's Le Le."

Lior had never seen anything so dazzling. Le Le was a very quiet dragon; she smiled at Athanus.

"She works hard," he explained, "Guarding the crystal mines from intruders. She will need to sleep."

Lior wanted to ask Athanus more questions, but everyone seemed to be settling down to sleep. More dragons appeared, looking tired and ready for a nap. They joined the huddle beneath the trees, some greeting each other with nods or gentle nuzzles before laying down.

A dragon with the muscular body of a man approached Athanus. He stood on two legs, like Monty, but had an enormous thick tail, the size of a tree trunk. His head looked like a frog with a long beak. He had staring yellow eyes.

"Brought us a snack, have you, Ath?" he laughed loudly, making the other dragons urge for him to be quiet.

"Don't be barbaric, Pendra. Lior here is a guest."

Pendra laughed and flicked his long, forked tongue out in a quick hiss before wandering away again. Lior felt too afraid to sleep, now. Athanus closed his huge eyes and said,

"Come and sleep closer to me. Less chance of someone waking you up."

Lior did as he was told. He turned his head away from the daylight and the other dragons, pressing his forehead into Athanus' chest. Athanus grasped Lior's back in his enormous claw-like fins. It made a kind of cage and Lior felt safer than he'd ever felt in his life. He closed his eyes and allowed the music of the deep dragon breaths all around him to lull him into a deep sleep.

Lior was woken up by a gentle wash of light over his closed eyelids. He looked up blearily to find himself in his own bed, his Dad gently removing the pillow Lior had pushed his face into.

"Hey, you," Dad said, "How are you feeling?"

"Can I go to school?" The first thing on Lior's mind was hearing the end of the story.

"I'm sorry, love, school's finished. You've slept all day! Do you feel better?"

"A little better," Lior had to admit he was still feeling quite achey and hot.

"Good. I think you could use some more rest, though. Mum's sent a message asking what you'd like to eat. Anything you want, since you haven't had anything all day."

Lior answered very quickly, "Vanilla ice cream with cherries and chocolate?"

Dad laughed, "If you have a sandwich now, I'm pretty sure we can arrange that for you, sir."

Dad left to answer Mum's message. Lior looked out of the window mournfully. His friends would be outdoors playing, now. He felt so tired still, but he didn't feel like falling back to sleep. He gave a dry cough and wondered how Ms McEwan's story had ended.

Hana swept into the room with a big glass of water and a book,

"Drink this. Are you up for a story?" Lior sighed and took a sip obediently. He was thirsty but he wasn't sure about the story. He was very bored, but Hana liked to read fashion magazines and books about dead artists or historical queens. He tried to think of a way to say now, when she showed him the cover of the book she held,

"*The Land of Dragons*!? Where did you get that?"
Hanah laughed, "I popped into your school on my walk home from *my* school today. Ms McEwan is very lovely, she was asking how you were. I told her how sad you were to miss the story, so... here we are!"

"I had a dream, I think, about the dragons," Lior watched Hana carefully, to see if she might laugh at him.

"Great!" she answered, "There is only one chapter left in this book, so once we've read that you can tell me about your dream and maybe we can make our own story!"

She hopped onto Lior's bed and crossed her legs as she opened the book.

"Ready?"

"Absolutely."

Hana read from *The Land of the Dragons* while Lior listened, looking forward to the ice cream his mum had promised to bring home.

Through the Fence

Mia was bored. It was the summer holidays and she was stuck at home *all the time*. Summer holidays usually meant trips to the beach, castles, parks, relatives and friends houses. In the summer holiday Mia's parents usually took her for picnics and to climb up hills or to visit art galleries or feed the ducks in the pond. During every other summer holiday, Mia, Mum and Dad had gone for long drives, practised swimming, listened to music outdoors and had lots and lots of fun together.

This summer holiday was different. This summer holiday Mum and Dad were very busy. Not busy taking Mia places with them, but busy with a brand new baby. The baby was a boy. He was very small, with no hair and enormous blue eyes. He was very cute, and Mia loved to see him laugh or smile and she really liked it when he grabbed hold of her finger. The brand new baby, Mia's brand new brother, was called Oscar. Oscar cried. Oscar cried very loudly and Oscar cried *a lot.*

He always needed something. To be fed by his Mum, or by Dad from a bottle; to have his smelly nappy changed; to be sung a song or read a story; to be winded or just held close so he could fall asleep. Even when he was asleep, everyone had to creep around the house very, very quietly so that he wouldn't wake up and scream. Mum and Dad often took it in turns to sleep while Oscar was sleeping and whoever was awake *still* didn't have time to play with Mia. They would be washing clothes and doing the dishes and cooking meals and cleaning.

Mia tried to help. Mum and Dad usually showed her how to join in with cleaning, or how to chop up vegetables or measure ingredients for dinner. But now, they always told her they didn't have time. They urged her to go off and play. For the first few days, Mia was happy to play on her own. But, before long, she'd read all of her books. She'd completed all of her jigsaws- some more than once. She'd tidied up her bedroom, run down the batteries in her toy car and figured out that it was really too boring to play 'snap' on her own.

The weather was nice, so Mia played outside. There were no other children in Mia's street, so she played by herself. She lived in the last house on the very end of the street; their garden was the smallest. It had a little square of slabs, which Mia covered in chalk drawings of flowers and fairies and dragons and unicorns and stars. She'd become excellent at skipping and hopscotch. She was practising throwing and catching a tennis ball, sometimes bouncing it hard on the ground, sometimes throwing it hard in the air, when she made a discovery.

She bounced the ball off the fence, and one of the slats of wood swung to and fro. It was loose at the bottom. Mia gently pushed the wobbly slat to one side, being careful not to get splinters in her fingers, and saw something fantastic. Something she'd never seen before and never imagined would be right next to her own garden. Through the break in the fence, Mia saw a jungle.

The people who'd lived in the house next door had moved away more than a year ago. Mum and Dad often complained that, now they were gone, they didn't know any of their neighbours. Mia just wished there were other children to play with. Or, at least one other child. Technically, now Oscar had been born, there was another child, but Mia didn't know how long it would take for him to be the right size to play games with her.

Although Mia didn't have anyone else to play with, anyone to share her new discovery with, she knew that her summer holiday was going to be much more fun. She had a whole jungle to play in! Unlike her garden, the jungle through the fence had patches of long, long grass that whispered as it swayed in the wind. There was a weedy patch, springy moss studded with dandelions. There were several enormous, leafy green bushes. The long grass was wonderful for creeping through; Mia would hide there silently and saw all kinds of butterflies and birds- she once spotted a tiny mouse from her hiding place. Mia loved to lie on the soft patch of moss, looking up at the clouds scuffing across the sky. She would choose three or four and decide what they looked like; animals, boats, castles, fairies, people, fruit. Then she would turn herself upside down and decide what they looked like once she changed her perspective. She could play this game for a long, long time. The overgrown bushes were great for exploring and Mia would climb over and under their long branches to make her way through the middle. At night, when she was in bed, Mia could hear the loose fence slat banging, if the wind rattled it. It made her smile.

There were no flowers in the garden, but there was a fence on each side. One hot day when there were no clouds and all the animals seemed to be hiding from the sunshine, Mia brought her chalks through the hole in the fence. She wanted to decorate it with flowers. She began by drawing long green stems and brightly-coloured petals. Before long, she began to use the bumps and knots in the wood of the fence for inspiration; from the shape of an eye she drew a dragon; from a bump that looked like a diamond, she drew a fairy princess; she found a series of tiny holes, which began the bubbles rising from the mouth of a rainbow fish.

When she was finished, almost all of her chalk was gone- she had one long white piece left. A few nights later, it rained very, very heavily. Mia went out to play to find that the chalk drawings on her slabs were all gone. She assumed the fence would be cleaned, too. However, when she visited the jungle that day, she discovered that the chalk drawings were still there! The rain couldn't touch the fence, because it was standing straight and upright. Mia worried for a moment but soon forgot about it. No one lived in the house at the top of the jungle, anyway.

Every evening, Mum or Dad would call, "Mia! Come for dinner!" and Mia would scurry through the fence like a rabbit and run to the table. Sometimes Mum or Dad would comment that her clothes were very dirty, or ask how she got pieces of grass stuck in her hair. Mia would shrug and they would send her to wash her hands. One day, Mia was playing in the jungle and didn't hear the call for dinner. She was exploring a long, thin spider web built between two sturdy blades of grass. Sitting proudly beside her creation was a light brown spider with striped black and brown legs. Mia had watched the spider finish off her web and was very impressed. She was talking quietly to the spider when she heard a very loud voice say, " Mia? Where have you got to?!"

Her Dad sounded worried so she hopped out of the grass quick as a rabbit and wriggled through the fence. She had to pause to unhook herself as, in her haste, she'd caught her t-shirt on a nail in the fence. She smiled at Dad and began to skip towards the door, but Dad was not happy,

"Mia? Come back here," Dad was looking between the wobbly fence slat and his daughter, "You've not to do that! You could get hurt, there are sharp things in that fence. And who knows what could be in an overgrown garden? It's not safe. Stay in here from now on, okay?"

Mia looked around. They're garden seemed tinier than ever after exploring the jungle. She wanted to argue, to show Dad it was safe. She wanted him to explore the jungle with her. But when she answered, all she said was, "Okay, Dad. Sorry." He looked very tired, so she went off to wash her hands and eat dinner.

So, once again, Mia was confined to playing on her own in the garden. She became bored very quickly. She tried to make up some new games, but it was hard to think of things to play on her own. Dad brought her back a new book from his trip to the shops one day; for two days, Mia lay in the garden and read for hours, transported far away. But, it was over all too quickly. She read it again, and then there really was nothing else to do. The second time she finished the book, she lay down and closed her eyes and imagined she was playing in the jungle. She would stalk through the long grass and roll on her squashy patch of moss and look in the damp soil under the bushes for snails. Mia closed her eyes tight and balled up her fists and imagined as heard as she could. In fact, she imagined so hard she felt as though she could hear herself playing through the fence.

Mia opened her eyes, but the sound continued. She glanced at the kitchen window, but it didn't look like Mum or Dad were in there. She crept to the fence and put her ear against the little patch of holes. There *was* a noise in the garden. What could it be? Mia sat down to think. What if it was a lost cat or dog or tortoise? What if it was a burglar trying to creep into someone's house? What if it was an explorer from the other side of the fence? Mia knew she would get into trouble if her Dad caught her going back to the jungle. She looked around, and saw her book, her ball, her one piece of chalk and her skipping rope. She decided to go through the fence once again.

She snuck through the gap in the fence as quietly as possible. When she was on the other side, she dove into the long grass. There was definitely someone or something in the jungle with her. Mia held her breath and listened as hard as she could. She could hear breathing, shallow and fast breathing. Mia wondered what kind of animal breathed like that- a dog, maybe? Suddenly, Mia felt afraid. What if the thing in the jungle with her was a tiger? Or a wolf? Or... something even worse?!

Mia told herself to be brave, counted to three and sprang up out of the grass. The creature fell to the ground with a startled cry. After a moment, the creature sat back up, and Mia saw that it was a girl. A girl about her age. Whose breathing had been shallow because she was scared, too.

Mia sat a few feet away from the girl. She had enormous, dark brown eyes with long black eyelashes. She wore a long, square shaped dress that was a very pretty shade of red, and strappy brown sandals. She had dark skin, much darker than Mia's. She didn't look like anyone Mia had ever seen before. She looked up at the house, to see that curtains had been hung in the windows facing the garden. Mia's jungle disappeared before her eyes. It was just a garden, a garden which now belonged to someone else. She wanted to cry and she was scared the girl would be angry at Mia for climbing in through the fence. She was sure she was going to get into trouble now.

"Hello," Mia said quietly, "I'm Mia. Do you live here now?"

The girl didn't answer Mia right away. Mia was worried she was going to shout for her parents to tell them there was an intruder in the garden, or tell her to go away. Eventually, the girl said, "My name is Salwa."

Salwa has a very thick accent that Mia has never heard before. She's never heard the name Salwa, either and she could tell that Salwa doesn't know what to say to her. Just then, she heard Mum's voice calling her for dinner. Mia ran off, without saying goodbye, scared of being caught going out of the garden after Dad told her not to. Once she got safely to the door, however, she had a thought. She ran back onto the slabs and slid her ball, her skipping rope and her last piece of chalk over the fence. After a second of thought, she slid her book through the gap in the fence before going inside to eat.

The next day it rained and rained. Mia stayed inside and watched TV. Mum was working hard on her laptop, but when she had a break to feed the baby and have a sleep, she let Mia play a game on her computer. Once Mum was back to doing her work, Mia did some drawings. She drew some of the things she'd drawn on the fence in her jungle-dragons and fairies and flowers. But, it wasn't her jungle anymore. It was Salwa's garden. Mia coloured in her drawings, while hoping that Salwa had taken her book inside, so it wouldn't get wet in the rain.

The next day, it was dry enough for Mia to play in the garden. As soon as she thought it was safe, she ducked through the fence once again to search for Salwa. She wasn't in the garden. Mia looked in the grass and under all the bushes and couldn't find her anywhere. The grass was still very wet from the rain the day before and she couldn't sit down without getting soaked. Just as Mia was about to give up and sneak back onto her side of the fence, Salwa appeared. She was holding something colourful.

When she reached Mia, she smiled and said, "Hello!" and spread out the colourful thing she was carrying. It was a picnic blanket, a special one with waterproof underneath so the top would stay dry on the damp ground. Salwa slipped off her soggy sandals and sat on the blanket. She motioned with her hands for Mia to sit down, too. Mia was a bit embarrassed at the holed in her socks after she pushed off her trainers. But at least they were nice and dry.

Mia felt pleased, but very shy. Salwa had obviously been waiting for her to appear and wanted to see her again. But Salwa was very quiet. She hardly said anything! Just as Mia was wondering what to say next, someone else came into the garden. A woman who looked just like Salwa, but taller with longer hair. She smiled a great big smile. She wore red lipstick, a bit like Mum's, which made Mia feel safer. She turned to Salwa, "Your mum?" she asked. Salwa didn't reply, but the woman laughed loudly. "You are Mia? I am Salwa's sister, Malika. It's nice to meet you."

Malika flopped down beside the girls on the mat, "Salwa told me about you. We moved here very recently, from Syria. Where we lived was near a war zone. We flew here to live somewhere safer."
Malika said all of this very calmly, but Mia was very shocked. She looked at Salwa, but she was listening to her sister, "Salwa doesn't know very much English- just a little so far. But she will learn, soon."

Salwa smiled and nodded her head, "Do you go to the school nearby? Salwa will go there after the summer." It was Mia's turn to nod.

Malika laughed, "You two are so funny," she nodded her head, making fun of them, "I don't think you'll be quiet for long..." Salwa and Mia smiled at each other. Mia wanted to make her feel welcome. She couldn't imagine having to move to a different country, where everyone spoke a different language. "Did you do these?" Malika was pointed at the chalk drawings on the fence slats. Mia bit her lip as she nodded her head, worried she was going to get into trouble. She thought about lying, but she knew she'd be caught as no one else had been in the jungle-garden.

"No one lived here for ages and ages, I didn't know you'd be coming!" Malika didn't look angry, though. She was still smiling.

"They're great," she said. "Now, we need to go to the shops today, will you be around tomorrow maybe?" Mia nodded and explained, "Mum and Dad just had a baby. We don't go out very much right now." Malika smiled sympathetically, "Ah, I remember that," and she gave Salwa a playful tickle. Malika laughed when she saw Mia duck through the broken fence, and she heard her voice chatting to Salwa in their language as they headed back into the house.

The next day, Salwa appeared in the garden with a huge smile on her face. She had brand new trainers on, very similar to the ones Mia wore, "Wow, they're cool, I like them!" Mia told her.

Salwa nodded, "Cool," she repeated. Mia laughed; Malika had obviously been teaching Salwa important English words. Malika showed up with a carrier bag full of something. Mia thought that maybe they'd do some tidying up of the garden. She didn't really like tidying up that much, but she *had* been playing in here a lot, so it seemed fair.

But Malika's bag had a surprise inside. Little pots of very brightly coloured paint. There were lots of brushes too, all different sizes. Some were brand new but some had clearly been used many times before. Salwa pointed at her sister and told Mia, "Artist." She looked very proud. Malika laughed and said, "Yes, I love art. Drawing and painting. I like building things, too. Anyway. I love these drawings you've done, Mia," she gestured to Mia's artwork, "But they are not going to last long if they're just in chalk. I thought we could make them last a bit longer."

Malika showed Mia and Salwa how to outline Mia's drawings using a small paintbrush. She taught them the right sized paint brush to use for colouring in the different shapes and sizes. The paints were bold and bright and the drawings looked dazzling in the sunlight. Malika was working on colouring in a purple dragon, carefully doing the spikes along his back in orange, when Mia suddenly thought to ask, "Won't you get into trouble? From your Mum? For painting on the fence?" Mia could tell Malika wasn't sure exactly what she'd asked, but she quickly figured it out from the expression on Mia's face and she smiled reassuringly.

"We didn't have a garden at home. Just a very small house, no place to go outside. Mum will be happy we're making the garden our place." Mia smiled back. It *did* look pretty good, once the pictures were tidied up a bit and painted pretty colours.

It took the three of them three days to do both of the fences. In between Mia's drawings, Malika showed the girls how to paint stars and planets and patterns in the gaps in between. It looked pretty amazing, and when Mia washed her hands that evening, she felt happy as she watched the paint from her hands pour down the drain. She smiled happily to herself as she ate. When she was finished and Mum started doing the dishes, Dad said, "Oh, when I was going to the shop earlier, I saw something next door. It looks like someone's moved in!"
"Great!" Mum looked genuinely pleased, "Oh, I hope they're nice people." Mia was about to tell Mum and Dad all about the people who'd moved in next door - not that she'd met Salwa's parents but she was sure they were as nice as they're children - but Dad didn't let her speak.

"Mia, that means *definitely* no sneaking through that fence. That belongs to someone else now, and you've not to go in there. Do you hear me?"

Mia knew it was time to explain. She hadn't kept Salwa and Malika a secret on purpose- Mum and Dad had just been too busy to listen to her story. She took a deep breath and began,

"Dad-" but she was interrupted by a loud crying from the next room. Dad repeated, "Do you hear me, Mia?" over his shoulder as he marched to the living room to look after Oscar. Mia said yes but felt like she was going to cry.

She ran upstairs to her bedroom, and heard her Mum say,

"Of course she's upset, she's had no attention for weeks while this little one steals it all!" She didn't hear what Dad said in reply. She stayed in her room all night, practising drawing stars the way Malika showed her. When Dad came in to wish her goodnight, she pretended she was already asleep. She tried to figure out the best way to tell Mum and Dad about Salwa but they were always so busy. And they might be really angry if she told them how often she'd been there after Dad told her not to go. She decided she would ask Malika about it tomorrow- she would know what to do. It was very windy that night and Mia fell asleep listening out for the sound of her fence slat banging in the wind. She couldn't hear it. *That's strange*, was the last thing she thought before she finally fell asleep.

The next morning, after Mia had eaten some cereal, Dad said, "Mia, I forgot to get eggs at the shop yesterday. Why don't you come along with me for a drive in the car?" Mia's shoulders slumped, "Okay," she answered. She didn't want to go in the car, she wanted to go next door! While Mum and Dad were looking in the fridge, discussing whether or not they might need anything other than eggs, Mia ran outside into the garden. She planned to tell Salwa she'd be back later, or leave a message somehow. She rushed to the fence. But when she pushed the wobbly slat to the side- nothing. She tried all over them, thinking she'd somehow gotten mixed up and pushed the wrong one. But she hadn't. Mia realised what had happened. Dad had fixed the fence, so she couldn't climb through anymore.

Mia was so sad that she sat down in the garden and cried. She heard Dad calling her name, and began to dry her face. Before she could get back to the house, the doorbell rang. The doorbell hardly ever rang at the moment- they'd had lots of friends to visit before but Mum and Dad were very busy with the new baby and Mum promised them all on the phone she'd see them when Oscar was a little older. Mum ran off to answer the door and then called through the house, "Mia, I think it's for you!"

On the doorstep stood Salwa and Malika and a woman Mia had never seen before. She had a beautiful, bright dress on and a scarf covering her hair that matched. But Mia could tell by her eyes that she was Salwa's Mum. She was holding an enormous tray of something that smelled very, very sweet. And she was smiling,

"Hi," said Malika, while Salwa and their Mum nodded and said, "Hello, hello."

"I guess Mia hasn't got around to telling you about us yet!" Malika launched into the whole story, while Mum gestured them all to come inside and Dad began making coffee. He had to rinse out the nice coffee mugs, which had become dusty with disuse.

Mia could see that her Mum and Dad were delighted to have visitors. They were a little embarrassed that the house was untidy at first, but Malika shook her head and said, "Mum has us, she knows what it's like having a small baby!" And everyone laughed. Malika explained more to Mum and Dad about the war in Syria than she had to Mia, and her Mum, whose name was Rola, dabbed at her eyes with a tissue when Malika mentioned their Dad, who was still in Syria and hoping to join his family in their new house soon.

They all drank coffee together - while Mia and Salwa drank orange juice - and ate the delicious sticky pastries. After Malika told Mum and Dad all about her family, Mum and Dad told them a little about theirs. Rola told Mum that she didn't know as many English words as Malika but Mum waved her hand and said she'd soon learn and not to worry. From that point, Mia was allowed to play in the garden next door whenever she wanted. Where the wobbly fence slat had been, Malika built a gate in the fence between the two houses, with some help from Salwa and Mia of course. After Mum and Dad saw their artwork on the fence, they asked the girls to paint Oscar's new bedroom, which he would move into when he was old enough. They covered it the same way they had done the fence. Then they did the bedroom Malika and Salwa shared, Malika drawing out a beautiful, intricate pattern on the wall, the girls colouring it in very neatly with tiny brushes.

They played and worked and ate together all Summer. Dad helped Rola in the garden, cutting the wild grass and pruning the bushes and tidying up some of the mess. Just before school started again, Rola got a letter telling them her husband would be home by the end of the year and they all danced together in the garden and had a barbeque for dinner to celebrate. As they ate food and sat on the grass in the late sunshine, Mia looked around at what had once had been her jungle. She saw her Mum smiling with her brother in her arms, not quite so tired all the time now. She saw Dad laughing and joking with everyone while he cooked. She saw the new friends she'd made, Malika constantly chatting and Rola absorbing every word everyone said and practising the language of their new home. Mia lay down on the springy patch of moss and pointed at the clouds, telling Salwa what she thought they looked like while everyone laughed together in the garden.

The Fire

Mark's neighbour, Mrs Abernethy, did not seem to like him. His Mum had always told him that it was polite to say, "hello!" to any of the neighbours if he saw them in the street, but every time he said hello to Mrs Abernethy, she completely ignored him. One day, him and his Dad were coming back from a walk late in the evening - they'd been trying to spot bats together in the trees in the park - and Mark could see Mrs Abernethy sitting in a chair in her living room. He noticed her because the light from her television was making her face change all different colours as she watched. She turned and saw him looking at her through the window as he walked down the street. He lifted a hand and waved. He gave Mrs Abernethy his biggest smile. Mrs Abernethy got up from her chair, leaned over to the window and pulled her blinds shut with a *snap*. It made Mark jump. *Well, that confirms it*, he thought to himself, *she really does hate me.*

One day, Mark was playing with his cousin Katie in the garden. They were practising football; both of them were on the school team and they practised shooting goals and passing the ball to one another. It had been raining, and they were both streaked with mud. Mum had told them to stay outside until they were finished playing football and not to come into the house until they were ready to get washed and changed into clothes that weren't soaked in mud.

She gave them both a bottle of water, packets of crisps and an orange and an apple. Mark was focusing on peeling his orange when Katie kicked the ball high in the air. Mark noticed at the very last possible moment, and he jumped in the air to headbutt the ball. The ball sailed into the sky as Katie and Mark cheered. When they stopped cheering, Mark asked,

"Where did the ball go? I was too busy celebrating to see it come back down!"

"I'm not absolutely sure either… but I think it must have gone over the fence and into next door's garden." Katie shrugged her shoulders.

Mark felt himself grow cold as the smile left his face. He couldn't see over the high fence and there was nothing to stand on, but he did find a gap just big enough to peek through. He couldn't see his ball but he could see one of the windows at the back of Mrs Abernethy's house. It had a big, round, dripping, muddy *splat,* right in the middle. There could be no other explanation. The ball was in her garden and he had headered it right into one of her windows.
"Can't see it," was all he told Katie.
"Show me which house it is, round the front, and I'll knock on the door and ask."

Mark looked at Katie. She was as muddy and wet as he was. He shook his head,

"She's probably not in right now. Let's get cleaned up and do something inside now. We've been playing for ages. I'll get it later."

Luckily, Katie raced off towards the house, shouting, "I'm picking what we watch on the telly!" She didn't mention the football again, but Mark felt guilty all afternoon. That night in bed it took him a long time to fall asleep, as he thought about Mrs Abernethy and the football.

The next morning, Mark was eating cereal at the kitchen table. His Dad came in from hanging out the washing and held up a weird, lumpy thing to Mark.

"What's this all about, Mark?"

Mark shrugged, "What *is* it, Dad?"

Dad sat down. His face was serious. Mark stopped eating his cereal.

"Well... it's a football. Your football. Did you and Katie do this yesterday? Something very sharp has punctured this ball. What did you use?"

"Where... where did you-"

"Mark. You left it right in the middle of the garden! How could I have missed it, I practically tripped over the thing to get to the washing line!"

Mark began to cry. It took Dad a few minutes to realise that Mark hadn't punctured the ball after all. When he was finished, he exclaimed, "She *hates* me!"

Mum came into the kitchen, her pyjamas still rumpled from bed, carrying her reading glasses and a very thick book, "Who hates you Mark?! Surely that's impossible," she reached down to ruffle his hair but stopped smiling when she noticed his tears, "What's going on?" her voice sounded very serious. Dad sighed and lifted up the sad, saggy shape that had once been Mark's football.

Mark stopped crying and said, "Mum, it was an accident. I headed the ball into Mrs Abernethy's garden and she punctured it and threw it back over the fence and she hates me, she never ever smiles at me or says hello!"

Mum nodded as she listened, then she began bustling about the kitchen,

"Have you had breakfast, boys? Who wanted kippers and eggs?"

Dad put the squashed ball under the table, washed his hands and put on the kettle. Mark screwed up his face, "Just an egg for me please, Mum."

Every Saturday morning, Mum would lie in bed reading a book while Dad did some of the housework. Then she'd get up and cook breakfast for them both- it was usually kippers and eggs, Dad's favourite breakfast. Mark hated the smell of kippers but Dad never complained when he ate lime jelly, even though it made him feel sick, so Mark stayed quiet about it.

One person *did*, however, like the smell of kippers, very much so. As Mum began cooking, a ginger tabby cat slinked her way through the cat flap. The cat flap had been in the door when Mum and Dad and Mark had moved in, but Mum wouldn't let Mark get a cat of his own. She said that he wasn't old enough for the responsibility of looking after an animal. The cat hopped onto Mark's knee,

"Hello, Eddie," Mark said as he stroked her softly. She began to purr. He rested one cheek very gently on her back and the purring became even louder. The cat used to have a little metal tag on her collar which said EDITH. It had disappeared a while ago, probably fallen off. Mark had always called her Eddie, after mispronouncing the name on her collar. His reading had improved quite a bit since then.

Eddie liked to have a little bite of kippers and eggs and she always came into the kitchen once she smelt the kippers cooking. Sometimes Mark saw her sitting on the fence in the garden, but he wasn't sure which house she lived in. He was pretty sure she would go anywhere she could smell good things to eat. On her weekly visits to Mark's house, she certainly walked around as though she owned the place. While Mark ate eggs and Mum, Dad and Eddie had some eggs and kippers, Mark asked,

"Do you think I could write Mrs Abernethy a note? To say sorry? We learned in school about people in the 18th century writing letters to each other all the time, even to people who lived just down the street…"

"I don't think Mrs Abernethy is quite *that* old," Dad laughed, "But that might be a nice idea."

"Hmm," Mum was frowning, "I'm not sure. If she'd come to us to complain or had given you a row, then perhaps. But she ruined your football. I think we might have passed the apology letter stage."

Mark looked sadly at his empty plate. Eddie was purring in his lap, delighted with her second breakfast.

"I don't see how it could make things worse, though," Dad was nodding in agreement with Mum, "So if that's what you want to do then go ahead. But just put it through her letter box, don't bother her."

The sun was shining outside but the garden was still quite soggy- running all over the grass with Katie yesterday hadn't helped. Mark sat on the doorstep and spent a long, long time writing his letter to Mrs Abernethy. He started over and over again, aiming for his best handwriting and perfect spelling. He even brought a dictionary outside with him to check his work. By dinner time, Mark had written a lovely note. It read:

Dear Mrs Abernethy,

I am so very sorry about the football hitting into your window. It was an accident and it won't happen again in the future. Please please please accept my apology. I am very sad that I have upset you.
From,

Mark who lives next door

(PS- I'm not upset about the football. I understand.)

Mark included a small illustration at the bottom, of him in a garden full of flowers with a very sad face. He showed his Mum and Dad and they agreed it was the nicest apology letter either of them had ever read. The next day, Mum and Dad were taking Mark to town to buy a new football. Mark planned to post his letter through Mrs Abernthy's letterbox before they left in the morning. Mark went to bed that night feeling much, much better. He was looking forward to getting up in the morning.

Mark's Dad woke him up very gently. He felt so tired! Was it morning already? Mark sat up, bleary-eyed. His room looked strange. Usually the sun woke him up as it came through the thin blue curtains, brightening up his whole room. But it was dark. Then Mark realised- it wasn't morning yet. It was the middle of the night.

"What's going on?" Mark asked. Dad's face looked very, worried. "Dad? Where's Mum? Is she okay?" "Yes, it's alright, Mark. Mum's outside. There's a fire. I said I'd stay here with you but I think we should go outside, just in case. Come on."

Mark thought about getting dressed but Dad seemed in a rush, with his hair all sticking up. It must be late enough that Mum and Dad were in bed, too, thought Mark. Then Mark heard sirens: fire engines. Without speaking, Dad and Mark rushed to the kitchen. Mark pushed his bare feet into his trainers at the back door and hoped he wouldn't be too cold in just his pyjamas as he followed Dad out the door and into the night.

It was not cold outside. In fact, it felt very hot. Mark realised that the fire must be quite big if it was heating up the street. He could smell it- it reminded him of something forgotten about in the oven, burning. He couldn't see it though. He looked around and realised there were people standing behind him, looking at something. Mrs Abernethy's house. Mark began to wonder why they were all looking that way until his sleepy brain caught up. Mrs Abernethy's house was on fire. Mark thought he was going to start crying. Dad took hold of his hand.

"Where's Mum?" Mark couldn't see her anywhere. Dad didn't reply. They both stood, watching the black plume of smoke rise from their neighbours house and into the sky. Mark couldn't see the fire, there was far too much smoke, but he could feel its heat. He could hear it too, crackling and sputtering inside the house.

"Dad, I can't see Mum *or* Mrs Abernethy. What's going on?" Dad didn't reply, just clung to Mark's hand and stared straight ahead, the same way everyone else was looking.

A huge cheer came from the small crowd and they all rushed forward.

"STAND BACK, STAND CLEAR EVERYONE," a huge voice boomed. When the crowd moved aside, Mark saw an enormous person in a rubber suit with a big helmet. He was holding two much, much smaller people in front of him and there was a horrible sound coming from them. Then Dad dropped Mark's hand and rushed forwards.

The fireman, the man in the rubber suit, was holding up Mrs Abernethy. Mum had her other arm. They all spoke together before Dad led them both to where Mark was watching. Mum and Dad were deep in discussion but Mrs Abernethy was making a horrible sound, a sort of wailing cry, repeating the same word over and over again.

"She's in shock," Mum told them gently. But Mark was listening more carefully than Mum or Dad or the fireman. Mark knew that Mrs Abernethy was saying, "*Edith!*" as she cried.

The fireman had told Mum and Dad to take Mrs Abernethy into their house until an ambulance came to check her for injuries, but she was struggling against them, trying to stay outside. The pieces of the puzzle fell into place for Mark. Edith was Mrs Abernethy's cat. And Mrs Abernethy was scared that Edith was trapped in the house. Mark stood on his tiptoes in his trainers and made his voice as big as possible,

"Mum-" Mum shook her head,

"Mark! Not now darling, this is an emergency!"
Mark was scared for his friend, too. His fear made his voice loud and strong, "Yes it is! Eddie might still be inside that house!"

Mum and Dad turned to Mrs Abernethy, both of them hearing for the first time what she had been repeating over and over. Mum's face looked very upset but Mark knew exactly what to do.

"Right, do we have any kippers?"

"What? Mark, we can't-"

"Mum. Cook kippers. Eddie will smell them. It's worth a try."

Mum ran back to the house. She pulled out four pans, one for each ring of the hob and went to the freezer. She put kippers in every pan and began poaching them all at the same time. In just a few moments, the kitchen began to smell very fishy indeed. After ten minutes, Mrs Abernethy and Dad could smell the kippers from outside. Mum didn't move from the hob, scared to leave the flames unattended, but stood staring at the open back door, her fists squeezed together.

Mrs Abernethy gave a shriek from outside. Eddie barrelled into the kitchen, wide eyed and terrified. Dad and Mrs Abernethy sat at the table. Dad was smiling and Mrs Abernethy was crying tears of joy. Everyone was safe from the fire.

That night, Mum drove Mrs Abernethy to a hotel a few miles away and Eddie the cat stayed in Mark's house for the night. After a few days, the damage to Mrs Abernethy's house was repaired and she and Eddie moved back in just like before. However, lots of things were not just like before. Mrs Abernethy no longer ignored Mark. In fact, they became very good friends. When Mark told her about Eddie visiting for kippers and eggs on a Saturday, she laughed and laughed,

"That's marvellous, a cat after my own heart, dropping in for a spot of breakfast! Do you know, I named her Edith as that was my own stage name, a long long time ago now, but I did know a chap named Eddie around that time who *did* love to eat kippers for his breakfast!"

Mrs Abernethy had a beautiful laugh, like a tinkling bell.

"Stage name? What is that?" Mark asked.

"Well. It's a name a performer uses, instead of their real one. I was a dancer."

"Most of the girls in my class go to dance lessons. Two of the boys do, too."

"*Everyone* should learn how to dance," Mrs Abernethy exclaimed, "But never mind about lessons, I'll teach you."

And she did. Mrs Abernethy taught Mark to dance and to play poker. She often came to visit for dinner and she came every Saturday morning, along with Edith, for kippers and eggs.

The Record-breaking Snowman

Tomasz woke up early. It was the last week of school before the Christmas holidays and he was excited. It had already begun to snow a few days earlier, just a few gentle flakes spinning from the sky, but his Dad said that the forecast was for heavy snow all through Christmas. Tomasz, like most children, loved the snow. He loved making snowballs, he loved building snowmen, he loved creating igloos and trying to hide inside them (although, to be honest, he had never been really successful at this quite yet).

He looked out his window and saw that the snow had become heavier during the night, while he had slept, In fact, it had become *much* heavier during the night. On the outside of his bedroom window was a big rim of snow, as thick as his hand! He could feel the cold pushing through the glass, reaching towards him. He huddled into his warm duvet and lay back down in bed. He dozed happily for another hour or so, the only light in his room coming from the street lights outside. When he heard his Dad's alarm go off next door he got dressed as quickly as possible in his school uniform, with his fluffy slippers on his feet to keep him cosy until it was time to leave.

He filled up and turned on the electric kettle and opened up the kitchen blinds while it boiled. He was in a daydream, looking out at all that perfect, untouched snow just waiting for him in the dark, when his dad turned on the light and made him jump.

"You're up very early! What's got into-" his dad stopped when he saw the snow, understanding immediately why Tomasz was up and dressed so early. His dad began to make Tomasz a hot chocolate, a treat he allowed on very cold days, and slid two slices of toast into the toaster while Tomasz laid out the plates and the knives and the butter and jam.

"When I was your age," his Dad continued, as he whisk the cocoa powder and sugar into the milk in the pan, "We had to walk two and a half miles to school, every day. And we had snow like this often in the Winter. There were no 'snow days' for us!"
"What's a 'snow day'?" Tomasz asked, hovering over the toaster, waiting for the bread to pop back out as lovely golden toast.

"Ahh... it's when the snow is so heavy that you don't go to school or work." Tomasz thought about it. It would be nice to play in the snow all day, but he saw most of his friends at school.

"Since you and I have a very short walk to go to school and to work, no snow days for us." said his

Dad. "If I stayed home, who'd buy the bread for toast?"

"Or this nice jam," Tomasz agreed, "Don't worry, if the school had to close, I know what to do."

His dad smiled, "Yes, Alicja." That was Tomasz's aunt. She lived four streets away from his house. She ran her own business, doing nail art from home. She was very good and whenever there was a parents' night or an after school event, Tomasz could recognise her artwork decorating the hands of a lot of the Mums, and some of the older sisters, who visited.

Tomasz' Dad worked as a mechanic, in a garage just a ten minute walk from their house. Tomasz's school was less than ten minutes walk, but in the other direction. They said goodbye at the front door. There were *lots* of children in the playground this morning, a lot more than usual. They were obviously desperate to play in the deep snow. He saw kids making snow angels, rolling up balls for snowmen and throwing great armfuls of the stuff at each other. Tomasz knelt down and made a snowball, his waterproof gloves still on. The snow was good - excellent in fact - for making snowballs. Tomasz tossed the snowball between his gloves as he wondered if this would be the year he finally managed to make a working igloo.

His thoughts were interrupted by a horrible, freezing sensation running from the top of his head, all the way down his back. He turned around to see Oliver grinning, his face flushed white on his nose and cheeks from the cold. He was peering out from an enormous hat. Tomasz threw his snowball with one hand and pulled Oliver's hat down to his chin with the other, rubbing freezing snow into his exposed neck. He shrieked,

"Stop, stop, truce!" he was shivering and laughing. Tomasz made him shake on his promise not to throw anymore snow at one another, and he relaxed after the deal had been made.

"Want to build an igloo?" Tomasz asked. He was hopeful Oliver would help him, he was the cleverest in the class. If anyone could make a good igloo, it'd be Oliver.

"I want to build a *gigantic* snowman," Oliver replied, his eyes shining with delight, "Last year, I made a pretty big snowman in the playground, but that bully Johnny Patterson came and smashed it all up."

Tomasz nodded as he listened. He'd only started at this school last February, so he hadn't been there. But he had seen Johnny Patterson, before he'd moved away to a new school and he'd heard lots of stories about him.

"Right then, it's agreed. There's no one here to smash it up. Let's make your snowman."

Everyone had grabbed all the best sheltered corners, so Tomasz and Oliver had no choice but to start building the snowman right in the middle of the playground. Both boys were quick and strong, so they had a good base started in just ten minutes. Oliver knelt down to pack the snow in tighter,

"This part's *really* important. If the base isn't sound, he'll toppled over before you get very high at all. Soon, other boys from their class had joined them, and some of the boys in the year below. Then, Aimee, who sat beside Oliver in the classroom, asked what they were doing. Aimee had lots of friends, and soon she convinced them all to help. By the time the bell rang to announce the start of lessons, almost two whole classes of children were working together. Now, Kingswood primary was very small. There were only about seventy pupils in the whole school, so everyone who came into the playground could see. They all went to class discussing the deep snow and hoping it would last over Christmas.

At break time, most of the children in the playground were either building the snowman, watching the snowman being built, or running around, throwing snow at each other and falling into heaps of it.

"Watch it!" Aimee shouted as two of the younger children almost ran into their mound of snow,

"We're trying to build *the biggest snowman ever.* So don't wreck it!"

By the end of break time, everyone knew about Oliver's plan to build a gigantic snowman- the biggest ever. Lots of them had carried armfuls of snow from all around the playground, heaping it up beside the snowman so the builders wouldn't run out. They even dismantled their own snowmen, to make sure there would be enough. When the bell rang, everyone promised they'd help again at lunchtime, to build the biggest snowman that had ever been seen.

After Maths, Tomasz and Oliver's class had art. Their teacher took everyone outside to look at the skyline of buildings and naked trees, so they could practise drawing a landscape from memory. She laughed when she saw the big mound of snow,

"That's almost all the snow in the playground!"

Oliver and Tomasz looked at each other, both realising at the same time that that's what they had to do. Use all the snow they could possibly get their hands on.

Everyone ate lunch quickly that day. The dinner ladies were astounded when all the plates were cleared and neatly stacked away minutes after they had served the children their food. They wondered what was going on, and asked the janitor,

"No idea," he replied, "But I'll find out. Nothing around here stays secret from me for long!" When he went outside, he saw what the children were doing. Now, he'd worked as a janitor for thirty years and, in that time, he'd seen quite a few playgrounds full of snow. He'd also seen quite a few children attempt to build a mega sized snowman- in fact, he thought he could recall trying it himself when he was in school. But never had he seen such progress made by halfway through lunchtime. All the children were working together, passing one another armfulls of snow. They had used almost all of it, but the head of the snowman wasn't finished yet!

The janitor got a shovel and his wheelbarrow and, as quickly as he could manage, shovelled the snow from the pavements outside the school into the wheelbarrow. When he dumped the new load of clean, white snow beside the snowman, all the children cheered.

"How far you got left to go? He had to look up to talk to Oliver and Tomasz, who were on top of the enormous mound of snow, shaping the body while children on the ground made the head.

"Not much," Oliver replied, "Once we've finished the head, we just need to get it up here!" The janitor nodded. He went to the staff car park. He'd shovelled the snow there early this morning, so the teachers could get into the building, but he'd left it in a big heap. He shovelled the snow from the car park into the wheelbarrow and took that to the children, too.

"Thank you, thank you!" seventy children all yelled and cheered at once. The janitor lifted up the completed head and raised it up so the boys could reach it, groaning under its enormous weight.

It was at that moment that the bell rang to signal the end of lunch break. There was a collective gasp from all the children. Then a voice from the door into the building called,

"Finish the job, everyone, before you come inside, please!" It was Tomasz and Oliver's teacher, smiling while she wrapped herself in her long cardigan and watched. With a final heave, The janitor got the head high enough for the boys to settle it onto the snowman's shoulders. They quickly packed snow around the neck to ensure it would stay on before everyone headed inside to go to class.

It was becoming dark again when the bell rang at home time. All the children gathered around the snowman before walking home or getting into cars and taxis. The janitor brought out a tall ladder and stretched out his palms to Oliver and Tomasz. They were full of buttons.

"Mind if I...?" the janitor asked.

"Of course not! He's everyone's snowman, you helped as much as anyone else here."

The janitor winked and climbed the ladder. The strongest boys and girls ran off to find arms for the snowman while everyone else watched. The janitor gave the snowman big eyes and a huge, bright smile. He stuck a pointy stone in the middle, which made a perfect nose. Before he climbed down, he took the dead branches the children had found and stuck them in deep, so the snowman would have two arms. They were excellent branches, strong and slightly bent in the middle, almost like elbows, with smaller twigs on the end mimicking fingers.

When the janitor climbed off the ladder, he stood back to see the full effect. Everyone cheered. It was the biggest, hugest, most ginormous snowman any of them had ever seen. Tomasz's Aunty Alicja had come to collect him and she stared with the rest of the parents. The teachers and some of the parents, including Alicja, took photographs on their phones, amazed by what the children had made together. Then they all hurried off, to finish marking tests or to make dinner for their family, or just to get home away from the cold. The children talked excitedly to one another, going home and telling younger or older siblings who hadn't been there what had happened. But the adults mostly forgot. Except for the janitor. He made a phone call before going home that night and he looked forward to the children finding out about his plan the following day.

The next morning, Oliver and his dad left the house early. Oliver had explained all about the snowman at dinner the night before, and his dad wanted to see it for himself. Alicja's photo wasn't quite enough evidence for him. But, as they got to the school, they found lots of people had had the same idea. There was a thick crowd of people all around the school. They couldn't all get into the playground, so they followed the fence all the way down until there was a space they could see through, into the playground.

Tomasz rubbed his eyes. He blinked them hard. He pinched himself. He couldn't believe that he was awake and seeing what he was seeing right before his very eyes. His dad laughed loudly beside him,

"It is a joke? Ha, how funny! You've fooled us all!"

There was no snowman in the playground. There was no sign of any snowman having ever been in the playground. In fact, the playground was now completely empty of any snow whatsoever. Tomasz couldn't believe it. Soon, Oliver joined him and his dad, who was still laughing,

"Now, boys," he said, "Tell the truth now, this is a big joke?" he winked at Oliver, but he shook his head, "No, it was real... I swear..."

All of the children were in shock but Oliver looked very, very upset. Tomasz remembered it'd been his idea in the first place and he gave his friend a hug, which was awkward in their bulky winter jackets.

Oliver gave a little smile, but he was still bewildered, "There must be some explanation, how can this have happened?" They all stood looking at the deserted playground until the bell rang. Tomasz and Oliver rushed to school, while parents rushed to work, including Tomasz's dad. When they were almost at their classroom, the janitor stopped them,

"What's going on, boys. How have you done it? I mean, it's *amazing* but... well... a bit embarrassing."

"I know," said Tomasz, "After everyone bragging about it, it's just... gone."

"He," corrected Oliver, "He, not it."

"Sorry," said Tomasz.

The janitor interrupted, "No, no, you don't understand. I invited the *Guiness of World Records!*"

Tomasz and Oliver stared, stunned, "You what?!" they said together.

"I called them last night. I mean, that had to be the biggest snowman anyone's ever seen, right? Surely. I just thought... well, I wanted... You all worked so hard."

The front doorbell buzzed angrily.

"Is that them now?!" Oliver asked.

"Right, off to class, boys, I'll handle this." The janitor looked nervous as he went to answer the door.

Tomasz and Oliver had almost forgotten about the visitor when the janitor found them at break time,

"Okay. The fella's still here. I managed to keep him here all morning. He's in the staffroom now having a cup of coffee and looking at the photographs some of the staff took. At least he won't think I'm just an out and out liar!"

The boys started to laugh, and soon the janitor joined in, too. The situation *was* ridiculous.

"Hang on, "Tomasz said, "Parents took pictures, too. Lots of pictures. Surely we have enough evidence to prove it?"

The janitor thought about it and nodded slowly, "Perhaps... perhaps..."

At lunch time, the man from the *Guiness Book of World Records* came into the lunch hall and the playground, asking the children about the snowman. Of course, they all told him the same story, the true story, of working together to build an enormous man made of snow and returning to school the next day to find him vanished.

When he eventually reached Tomasz and Oliver, the man had no idea what to think anymore,

"But how can this be?!" he demanded

"Well…" Oliver looked thoughtful. "He was here, we all saw him. And he hasn't fallen down; there's no snow in the playground. And he hasn't melted; it's still far too cold, and none of the snow in the gardens or the streets has melted at all. And we haven't made him up; you've seen photographic evidence. I can think of only one explanation."

"Me too," said Tomasz. He had no idea what Oliver was going to say, but he was very loyal to his friend. Plus, Oliver was *really* clever. He probably did know the answer.

"He must have… just… walked off." Oliver shrugged his shoulders. Tomasz nodded along, taking in what his best friend had just told the man.

The man didn't bother replying. He walked back into the building, talking to himself and shaking his head. The children talked about his visit, and the snowman, right up until the Christmas holidays. But they forgot all about that amidst the Christmas presents and lights and food and visits to family and the tonnes of snow that fell. When they all got back on the fifth of January, there was a notice attached to the notice board just outside the school. It was from the *Guiness Book of World Records.*

It read:

To everyone at Knightswood Primary school,

Thank you for your hospitality. I thoroughly enjoyed my visit. Unfortunately, I cannot enter your snowman into our records as the biggest ever, as no one from *The Guiness Book of World Records* witnessed it with their own eyes.

I can, however, inform you all that a new category will be entered into this year's book: an honorary mentions category. The first record in this category with be the following:

Record for the most children, staff and parents at one primary school convinced a man made of snow has walked away after his construction

This award, of course, will be awarded to Knightwood Primary school.

Have a wonderful new year,
Richard Clerk

Tomasz and Oliver read the notice four or five times, laughing harder each time they read.

"A new category," Tomasz said, "that's pretty amazing, Oliver."

"Yeah," Oliver agreed as they walked into the playground together, "Maybe next year we'll build an even bigger snowman…"

The Enchanted Tower

Once upon a time, a princess was trapped in a tall, tall tower. Her name was princess Althea. She had been cursed by a witch who was angry with the princess' father, the king, for chopping down a magical tree at the very end of her garden, right at the edge of the forest. He wanted to use the enchanted wood from the magical tree to build a bewitched fire that would burn for an entire week. The fire would be in celebration of the princess' eighteenth birthday.

The fire was lit seven days before the princess' birthday. However, before the celebrations began, the witch cast her spell and the princess found herself locked up in a very quiet room with only one window. The room was at the very top of a tall, tall tower. There was the one window to look out of, but no door to escape and the tower was far too tall to try to climb down.

The witch appeared to the terrified king in a cloud of smoke, inside the enchanted fire, and told him about the curse but she would not reveal where his daughter had been imprisoned. Everyone in the kingdom loved the princess; she was creative and kind, and painted murals all over the walls of the kingdom, with the help of the children. She planted things so the kingdom always smelled lovely and looked green and inviting. And she played her guitar at parties in the castle, where everyone in attendance would smile and sing along with her songs.

The kingdom loved their princess so much that everyone who had a horse rode all over the kingdom to try to find her. They searched everywhere, through the forests and over the river, on the top of hills and in the valleys. At the end of the week, the day that was the princess' eighteenth birthday, they wept when the magical fire finally fizzled out. The king wept most of all; everyone was sure they would never see the princess again. People whispered that she must have vanished or perhaps even been killed. It was a terrible loss to the kingdom, which became a dull and very sad place without her influence.

However, the princess was not vanished or dead, simply locked up in the tower under the curse. The witch had enchanted the tower so that no one would be able to see it or hear the princess' cries for help. The princess could see the people of her kingdom looking for her. She saw the children she played with searching for her alongside the king. But they could not see her and they could not hear her. The princess knew she'd be stuck inside the tower for the rest of her life.

Gradually, over the next few years as the witch grew older and weaker, the spell hiding the tower from view became weaker, too. Now someone might see the tower if they were to walk by. So, she encouraged enormous, spiked vines to grow. These were also magical, and parted only to allow the witch herself access through their prison. They were growing from the ground, so they would not weaken as she aged. If there had been any hope of escape for princess Althea, it dwindled away to nothing as the vines grew higher and higher.

In the next kingdom, prince Adam was arguing with his mother. Prince Adam had just celebrated his twentieth birthday and the queen thought it was time that he was married. She was looking forward to having a nice daughter in law and, hopefully, some grandchildren. She wasn't too worried about prince Adam having an heir to the throne, as she had a younger brother who was only thirty years old; once she died, he would take the throne, or perhaps one of his children. No, she didn't need an heir but she did long for a bigger family. Her husband, the king, had been older than her when they married and had died several years ago. The queen was lonely in the castle with very few people to talk to. So she wrote to the king and queen of the next kingdom to invite them and their daughter, princess Felicity, to the castle for a banquet. Princess Felicity was nineteen and, she had heard, very pretty. She crossed her fingers that her son would think she'd be a suitable wife.

But their meeting was a bit of a disaster. Prince Adam thought princess Felicity was very beautiful and she thought prince Adam was extremely handsome. They blushed at one another when they met, exchanging shy smiles, and their parents chatted amongst themselves while they ate, allowing their children to get to know one another. Prince Adam started to talk about where the delicious wine on the table had come from and where he had his lovely clothes made. He complimented Felicity on her dress and on her hairstyle. Felicity wasn't very interested in fancy food or fashion though. She was interested in reading and writing and playing music.

Adam could chat about all of these things, but quickly became annoyed when Felicity asked him about books he'd never heard of; she'd obviously read a lot more books than he had. They talked about writing; Adam had written letters to his friends and the occasional poem. Felicity wrote stories; she was hoping to write a whole book of stories one day. Adam began to wonder what it would be like to have a wife with such an ambition. She'd be very busy, he thought.

When the conversation turned to music, Adam boasted that he could play three instruments; the piano, the harp and the guitar. Felicity thought that sounded wonderful. When he asked if she played any instruments, her mother overheard and interrupted,

"Oh, Felicity just adores music! She plays almost everything; self taught, once she picks up an instrument a few times, she seems to know it like the back of her very own hand!"

Felicity turned bright red as everyone looked at her. She was really quite shy. Adam was a bit red, too. He realised the princess was entirely unsuitable as a wife. She spent too much time reading and playing instruments. That would never do. Finally, he asked,

"Can you knit, too, princess? Sew? Crochet?"

"No, I must admit I cannot prince Adam!" and he smiled, pleased he'd found something she could not do. His smile faded quickly, when she added, "Can you?"

Everyone at the table laughed when prince Adam shook his head. He decided he could not marry princess Felicity.

Once Felicity and her parents left that evening, Adam's mother was very excited. The queen was practically jumping with joy,

"Oh, *Adam!*" she cried as the door closed behind their guests, "What an absolutely wonderful girl! So talented and so clever. And very beautiful, too! And modest! Did you see how she blushed? What a wonderful wife she will make you. And your children would-"

"Mother." Adam interrupted the queen very firmly, "I will not be marrying that woman. She's... she's... entirely unsuitable! I don't want to hear about her again."

The queen was really, really, really disappointed. But when Adam added, "I can find a wife by myself," she felt a bit angry. She replied,

"Well, in fact, you *don't* seem to be able to find a wife at all! You're just too immature, I suppose. You never decide anything for yourself. If you had a wife, I wouldn't have to look after you so much!" and she flounced off, her long skirt train bobbing along behind her. Of course, she hadn't really *meant* what she'd said- she'd just felt upset. But Prince Adam didn't know that. He decided he would read *The Morning Star* at breakfast the next day. *The Morning Star* was the newspaper that reported stories from all of the five kingdoms. Yes, that's exactly what he'd do. He'd look in the paper at the stories and find himself a quest to embark on. Hopefully, a dangerous one. He'd see how his mother felt about *that.*

In the tower, the princess was very unhappy. The witch visited very rarely, to leave food and fresh water, and the rest of the time she was completely alone in the tower. There was no door to escape through, and so the princess sat at the high, high up window and breathed in the fresh air from the trees around her and tried not to look down at the frightening, twisty black vines. They seemed to grow higher every day. The princess watched the clouds go by as she brushed her hair, which had grown extremely long in the time she'd lived in the tower. She did have a pair of scissors in her writing desk, but she used her growing hair to mark how much time had passed. It reached the floor now. She hoped that one day the witch would notice how long she'd been trapped and let her go free.

Prince Adam cracked his spoon against his boiled egg with one hand and held *The Morning Star* in the other. He read all of the stories in the newspaper as he ate his egg and drank his tea. There was a dragon on the loose; dragons were mostly friendly if they were well fed and more or less left alone, but no one knew where this dragon had come from and the newspaper kept the people of all five kingdoms up to date with where he was last seen. Wolves had gone into hiding in one of the kingdoms, and there was a rumour that a huntress in a red cloak and hood had frightened them all so much that they were too afraid to come out during the day. There was a wishing well that needed repaired, an enchanted forest that needed volunteers for litter picking and someone was advertising jewelry made from the golden egg of a magical goose. And donating the profits to an enchanted wildlife charity.

None of the things reported in the newspaper seemed worthy of going on a quest. It had to be a *real* quest. A dangerous one, where he'd have to look after himself, that'd really show his mother. Then, prince Adam spotted a small article about seemingly enchanted vines growing in the forest in the kingdom next to his own- King Alfred's kingdom. His kingdom was a very sad place to visit- since the princess Althea had been kidnapped by a witch five years ago, when she was only eighteen, all of its people were sad. Hardly anyone visited them anymore. The vines, the article said, seemed to be hiding something, though it was impossible to tell what as they were so thick. Prince Adam closed the newspaper and poured himself more tea, nodding. Yes, that would be a quest worthy of a prince. To travel to that sat kingdom and solve the mystery of the vines. He'd be a hero. Probably. He finished his tea and snuck off to his room to get ready, before his mother could ask him what he was up to.

Prince Adam set off on his quest that very morning, hoping he'd be home in time for dinner, which was lasagne and one of his favourites. He rode out of the castle on Ivy, his fastest and strongest horse, and he headed towards King Alfred's kingdom to see what lay behind the vines.

The princess was growing more and more bored by the day. At first, she'd felt frightened in the tower, but after five years, she knew the witch wasn't going to hurt her. No, she was simply going to keep her locked up until she died of boredom. All because her dad had cut down the wrong tree. The princess couldn't help but feel a little bit annoyed with the

King. She didn't think he deserved to have his only child taken from him and locked up, but she *had* always been telling him to be careful about whose trees he cut down. He could be very careless about things like that. Kings often are; they're not used to being told 'no'. The princess sighed and brushed her long hair. Far away in the sky, she spotted the dragon she'd seen a few times recently. She longed for him to come closer so she could wave to him. And perhaps even ask him his name.

Prince Adam rode Ivy all day. At twilight, they'd only just reached King Alfred's kingdom and they were both exhausted. Prince Adam hadn't packed anything to eat except a couple of apples- he'd thought he'd have been back in his castle long before nightfall. He gave one of his apples to Ivy, who gobbled it down and sat down to eat the other one for dinner. It wasn't too cold a night and he was wearing a warm cloak. He lay down by a tree and, with nothing better to do until morning, fell fast asleep.

Prince Adam was woken up by a hard THUD, just before sunrise. At first, he thought Ivy had somehow fallen over. He whipped his neck around, but she was standing up. She did look very strange, though. She was staring dead ahead, at something behind him, seemingly petrified! Prince Adam realised that she hadn't made the THUD at all. There was something behind him. Probably something quite massive, if it had made a noise so loud it had woken him up. The brave Prince Adam held his breath as he turned around. And then he let out a not-very-brave noise that was very similar to a scream.

Peering down at him, almost as tall as the trees, was the dragon. The dragon from the newspaper. The dragon that might be very, very dangerous. prince Adam wanted to run away, or jump on Ivy's back and ride back home as fast as possible, but the dragon… the dragon didn't look very fierce after all… in fact, he looked… he almost looked a bit *sad.* The sun was beginning to come up and the soft colours reflected in the dragon's eyes.

The dragon had huge, teary eyes. Prince Adam forgot about being afraid,

"Why are you so sad, dragon? What's the matter?"

The dragon's reply in a rather quiet voice, for a dragon, "Oh, I'm just… well, I'm lonely. And hungry. Everyone I try to talk to runs away from me! I've tried to ask them where I can find something nice to eat but they won't listen to me! I ate a sheep last week and I've felt terrible about it ever since. He probably had a family!"

The poor dragon began to sob. He was huge and grand and he shimmered with magic, but he wasn't actually scary at all, once you got to know him. He was lonely.

"I'm really sorry, dragon," Adam replied, "I don't have any food at all. I haven't had any breakfast myself. I'm hungry, too!"

The dragon nodded politely.

"Say… you don't happen to know if a great mass of terrifying, spikey, knotted vines have grown near here? They're black, or very dark at least? Maybe look a bit enchanted?"

The dragon's face brightened. He was happy he could help,

"Why, yes! They're not far. Well, not far for me… about a hundred trees from where we're standing now. That way," he raised a wing to point prince Adam in the right direction.

Adam nodded and mounted Ivy,

"Do you mind if I tag along with you two?" the dragon asked, "Perhaps you could show me where I might find something to eat?"

The dragon walked quite slowly behind the prince and his horse. He was very weak with hunger. He was, however, excellent with directions, and they reached the tower just as the sun reached the blue sky.

"Oh my goodness," the prince uttered.

The vines were far more evil-looking and far thicker than he'd ever imagined. There was no way he could get through them to see what they were hiding! It occurred to prince Adam at that moment that he probably should have brought his sword. He was really quite badly prepared for his quest, with no food or sword. He wanted to go home and have a rest and a big lunch and try the quest another day, when he was properly ready. He could write off this time as a trial run. But, the dragon was here, too. He couldn't really abandon his quest with a witness watching him. He'd look like a coward!

Just as prince Adam was wondering how to get out of the pickle he'd gotten himself into, the dragon reached forward and took a massive MUNCH from the nearest vine. Adam was alarmed,

"You'll hurt yourself! What if it's poisonous!"

The dragon swallowed deeply, "I'm sorry, I was just so very very hungry. It probably would be poisonous to a prince but dragon's have very strong constitutions and, in fact," the dragon licked his lips thoughtfully, "That was actually rather delicious!"

He took another mighty munch and the Prince and Ivy watched, impressed at the dragons tremendous strength, and jealous he'd found something to eat. As they watched the dragon, a thought occurred to Adam,

"Dragon? I hope you are as hungry as you say you are... I think I have a plan."

The princess was just waking up inside the tower, the sun streaming through her window. She was so high up and the forest was so thick, she never saw the sunrise and she missed it. Five years, she thought, five years of no sunrises, no conversation, no company. No painting or reading. Just growing her hair and wishing she could go home. She sighed, and got up to brush her long hair. At least that took up most of the day.

She strained her ears as she thought she heard a strange noise. She *did* hear an unusual noise. She rushed to the window to investigate, sure the sound was coming from below the tower somewhere. What on Earth could it be? The sound grew louder and louder, but still princess Althea could see nothing but the thick, gnarled vines at the foot of the tower. They had grown truly enormous, now. She stared at them bleakly, wondering if they would eventually climb all the way to the top of the tower and into her window.

Just as her eyes filled with tears, she saw what was making the noise... far, far below, right on the ground there was... something. The princess squinted her eyes. Was it? How could it be? It *was,* it was a dragon! And he was... making the vines disappear. But how was that possible? The the princess called out,

"Are you eating those dangerous vines?!"

The dragon looked up at her. Dragons have excellent sight and excellent hearing. Prince Adam couldn't see what was at the top of the tower... but something seemed to be moving. Calmly, the dragon told him,

"It seems that there's a princess locked in that tower."

"A what?!" said Prince Adam, "I came here to solve the mystery of the vines, to find out why they were here and they're... they're... keeping a princess trapped in a tower?" Prince Adam was shocked. This really was a quest after all.

The dragon was less surprised, "Dear prince, why on Earth would someone go to all this trouble of magically growing these truly enormous vines, if they weren't hiding something extremely important?" Now the dragon was no longer weak with hunger, he was actually a bit cheeky. But, thought the prince, he did also have a point.

"Right. So. What do we do now?" Prince Adam asked the dragon. He turned to Ivy, too, in case she had any good ideas.

"I don't know! I'm only a dragon! I'll eat my way through this stuff and you make a plan. You're the prince, after all!"

Prince Adam thought very hard. He really had no idea what to do. Luckily for him, in her tower, the princess was cutting up her bed sheets and duvet, and the rug and the curtains. She cut up all of her clothes, except the nightdress she was wearing. She tied all of the long strips of material together with very strong knots and slipped the scissors into her pocket. She tied one end to the door handle and let the other hang from the window. She gulped as she looked down. It was *a long way to the ground.* And she didn't think her homemade rope would quite reach all the way. But she had to try. She hoped the dragon ate enough of the vines that she could escape.

The dragon munched and crunched, and prince Adam scratched his head as he thought, and the princess shimmied down the rope, using her feet to brace herself against the wall of the castle. She was quite unfit after having been locked in a single room for five years and soon she was out of breath and really very sweaty. But she was so happy to be making her escape, she had to try not to laugh with joy. When Ivy spotted the Princess climbing down the tower, she nudged the prince with her nose until he eventually looked up.

Prince Adam cheered. The Princess would be free! And he didn't need to come up with a rescue plan! He called up to her,

"There's a big jump from the end of your rope to the ground- we'll catch you!"

The princess couldn't reply, she was so breathless she could barely hang on. But she felt relieved. The dragon had almost cleared a path through the vines. However, at the moment, the rope took a massive lurch towards the ground and the Princess screamed in terror, convinced she would fall to her death. The dragon and Ivy and Adam all looked up, frozen. Then the witch appeared high up, at the window. She laughed a cruel, awful laugh and stepped on the end of the Princess' long, long hair, which hadn't all quite made it all the way out of the window yet.

There was a gasp of horror from below; the dragon and Ivy and prince Adam had made their way through, but the Princess was trapped again. Adam panicked, wishing he'd come up with a plan after all. But the princess knew what she had to do. She took the scissors from her pocket and she cut and chopped at the hair just above her head. She took a deep breath and let go of the rope. When she made the final *snip* she fell and fell towards the ground.

It was at that moment that the dragon, now full from his enormous snack, felt well enough to fly again. As the Princess fell he lifted himself up with a flap, flap, flap or his enormous wings, and she landed neatly in his back. He lowered himself gently as she rolled down his tail and landed, without injury, onto the grass that had been hidden beneath the vines for so long.

The princess had fainted from fear, convinced she was falling to her death. Prince Adam kneeled before her as she woke up,

"Hello. Are you alright there? You are... you are a princess, aren't you?"

"I'm free?" The princess was ignoring prince Adam, looking lovingly at her rescuer, the mighty dragon.

"You're free," he confirmed warmly.

"And you *are* a princess?" Prince Adam pressed on.

"Well... yes, I am. Or, I was. Before I was kidnapped on my eighteenth-"

"Ah, so you're *the* princess! How wonderful! I'm looking for a wife, you see."

The princess scowled, "First of all, it's really rude to interrupt someone when they're talking. And, secondly, I'm not going to be someone's *wife!* For a start we just met, I don't even know your name! And I've been *locked in a tower for five years.* I want to go home! I want to see my dad!"

Prince Adam nodded, "Let's get you home, then, princess. By the way, you don't happen to have anything to eat on you, do you, I haven't had any breakfast?"

The princess rolled her eyes and dusted herself off. She was very sore from climbing,

"You ride Ivy, I'll walk," Adam said.

"Thank you, I do appreciate that very much," she replied, "But what about you, dragon?"

The dragon said, "I've just eaten for the first time in weeks. I'll find somewhere to sleep quietly, and then I shall join you." They all agreed this was an excellent plan and set off towards home.

There was a huge party in the Kingdom that night. People came from all five kingdoms to celebrate princess Althea's homecoming. The dragon was the guest of honour and ate an enormous fancy salad with great delight. Princess Felicity met a book publisher who wanted to read her stories and make them into a book. Prince Adam met a lovely princess from the furthest away kingdom, who didn't play music or write books, but preferred sword fighting and climbing trees, things she promised to teach prince Adam. He thought that, if they got along well enough, she might make quite a good wife. And princess Althea was reunited with her father King Alfred, who promised never to cut down another tree without consulting her first. He admired her new short hairstyle as everyone feasted and danced together, delighted that princess Althea was home at last.

The Mystery of the Missing Hat

Daisy did lots of things every week. She went to school every day, she went to a dance class on a Tuesday, she went swimming with her dad on Thursdays. Sometimes she would go to a friends' house for tea, or if the weather was nice she would play in the garden. If the weather was bad she might play on the computer or read books or build with building blocks.

But Daisy's favourite thing to do every week happened on a Sunday. Every Sunday she would visit her Gran and her Grandad. Her Mum and Dad would go out for the afternoon, usually to do some shopping. Daisy would play with Grandad while Gran cooked a Sunday roast for everyone to eat together when Mum and Dad came home. Sometimes, one or two or ten of Daisy's cousins might be there. She had lots of aunts and uncles and her grandparents were friendly with all of their neighbours; they'd lived in the same house for many years. So, Sunday dinner was sometimes a very grand affair and it took Daisy's Gran all day to cook. She was never sure how many people would turn up! She had been the head chef of a very nice restaurant before she retired, so she enjoyed being in charge in the kitchen on Sundays.

The food was delicious, but that wasn't Daisy's favourite part of the day. She loved to play with Grandad. He would tell her hilarious made up stories, about elephants that could fly and talking post boxes and trees that grew chocolate Easter eggs on their branches. He would play hide and seek with her, in the garden if it was sunny and in the house if it was not. He showed her how to shoot a slingshot and how to blow bubbles with bubblegum and how to make a den out of sticks and leaves in the garden. Daisy did lots of lovely things every week, but her favourite part was spent racing around, laughing, joking and carrying on with her Grandad.

One Sunday, however, Grandad couldn't play.

"It's my dodgy knee, petal. Can hardly bend me leg! Now come here and let's have a story…"

Daisy enjoyed Grandad's stories as much as ever but she didn't like the way he hobbled when he had to get up to go to the toilet. She didn't like the pain on his face when he insisted on sitting at the table to eat, his leg stuck out very awkwardly beside him. He still stole potatoes from Daisy's plate and made faces at her to make her laugh, but he wasn't as happy as usual.

This went on for three more weeks. Then, one Sunday, Mum told Daisy,

"We aren't visiting your Gran's this week. Your Grandad managed to get himself bumped up the waiting list- you know how lucky he is. He's got a nice new knee now. All better!"

"When will I see him?" asked Daisy. She was very upset at the thought of her Grandad having an operation without her knowing about it. She hadn't had a chance to wish on her lucky sea shell that he would be okay.
"Ah, we'll still see him today, Daisy. At the hospital."
"Oh. Well, that's good. I've never been there."

Dad laughed, "You have so, you were born there! But you'll not remember that. Come on then, let's get to the car."

On the way to the hospital they stopped at the shop to buy Grandad some grapes, a box of chocolates and a magazine about cars. They parked in the car park and walked a long long way to get to the hospital doors. Then it was a long long way to walk to an enormous metal lift. And then it was a long long way down a long long corridor with squeaky floors. They walked past lots and lots of rooms.

"Not far now," Mum said with a smile.

"How did Grandad walk all this way with his dodgy leg?" Daisy couldn't imagine him hopping and hobbling all the way through the car park and into the lift and down all the corridors.

"He probably was in a wheelchair," Dad answered.

"This is it, ward 36," Mum pointed.

"What's a ward?" Daisy asked.

"You'll see one now!" Mum answered. But Daisy forgot to pay attention to the ward. Right at the other side of the big room they went into was Grandad, sitting beside a big window. Daisy ran to him, both of her parents telling her she had to walk in the hospital. But her Grandad was smiling so she kept going.

He pulled her up in his strong arms until she was sitting beside him on the bed. He was wearing a funny big blue shirt. Grandad almost never wore short sleeves, not even in summer. Daisy liked it because she could see the blue tattoo on his arm. She rubbed it and asked what it said.

"You know what it says... Doreen," he winked and Daisy turned around to smile at Gran, who was sitting in a plasticky looking green chair getting on with her knitting. She shook her head, but she was smiling, too.

The visit seemed very, very short to Daisy. There was hardly any time to play and when the nurse came to check on Grandad she told Daisy to get off the bed. She had an unfriendly face. They left soon after that and Daisy cried all the way into the big metal lift.

"Daisy, be calm," Dad said, "Grandad will be home, probably tomorrow. You'll see him next week."

"Home?" asked Daisy, "He's not staying in the hospital?"

Mum and Dad laughed, "No, darling. He's had his operation and they are just checking he's fit and healthy enough to go home. We'll be there with him next week."

Daisy felt much better knowing Grandad was going home. And she missed Sunday dinner at their house, but they got a takeaway curry instead, and that made Daisy feel better, too.

The next Sunday, they drove to Gran and Grandad's as usual. Daisy was very excited to see her Grandad without the grumpy nurse being there. It had been weeks and weeks since he could play with her properly and she couldn't wait to run about in the garden- it was a warm and sunny day.

When Mum parked outside the house, Daisy leapt out of the car and ran all the way round the back of the house to the garden. But Gran and Grandad weren't there. *That's strange*, Daisy thought, *they're usually sitting outside when the weather is nice.* She skipped into the house to find them. Gran was in the kitchen making cups of tea,

"Hello," Daisy said.

"Hello, love, how are you? Your Grandad's in his chair in the living room. Got the snooker on. He knows I prefer darts…"

Daisy found Grandad in his chair. His leg was propped up on a kitchen chair, straight out in front of him. And it was *HUGE*. All around the middle of his leg was a big puff of white bandages. Daisy gasped as her Grandad said hello.

"What's happened?" she asked. His leg didn't look fixed at all!

"It's alright, petal. It's just me bandages. This knee has to heal under all of these bandages and then it'll be back to me old tricks!"

Daisy was extremely disappointed but she tried not to show it. Poor Grandad.

He scooped Daisy up and squeezed her in beside him on his chair. It was a very squashy, soft and comfy chair and Daisy leaned back. She didn't like snooker either.

"What shall we do?" she said.

"Well, darling, you know… I just cannot find my hat *anywhere*. I think someone must have pinched it. But I had it this morning…"

"Have you gone out anywhere?" Daisy frowned. Grandad looked like he'd been sitting in the same spot for quite a while.

"No, I haven't. And no one has been in so… maybe your Gran stole it?!"

Daisy gasped, "No, she wouldn't do that! Where have you put it do you think?!"

Grandad wore his hat all the time. It was very strange to think of it as missing. Daisy always secretly thought that he probably slept in it! Where could it have gotten to?

"Well, there's only one other explanation, if my lovely wife hasn't pinched it… it's run off!"

Daisy wasn't sure if Grandad was serious or not. It was a silly idea, but his face looked really serious.

"Daisy, I'm going to have to trust you to hunt for my hat. Can you do that? Right now, I really need a helper."

"Of *course* I'll help you," Daisy jumped off the chair and began walking backwards and forwards in the living room, "But where on Earth might it *be*?" she asked as she walked. Her Grandad said,

"Right. We need to think like a hat that's off on an adventure… First, check under the bed. Then, check in the kitchen cupboards."

"Okay." Daisy sped off, happy she could help Grandad with something while he couldn't walk. She crawled under the big bed in the bedroom but there was no hat. There *was*, however, Daisy's favourite doll, Calliope. She took the doll to the living room and left her on the fireplace for later and then headed off for the kitchen. Gran was in there getting dinner ready. The kitchen was hot and steamy and it smelled delicious. Gran scooped Daisy up in a big cuddle while Daisy told her all about her mission to find the missing hat.

"Right," Gran nodded, "Let's get these cupboards checked."

Gran checked all the high up cupboards while Daisy checked the ones down low. They didn't find the hat, but they did find a nice, bright satsuma, a mini packet of Daisy's favourite chocolates and a packet of crisps. Daisy took the things she found back to the living room and put them beside Calliope and reported back to Grandad.

"Okay... let's think...let's think... where could he have got to... Right, next try behind those curtains over there and on the bookshelves in the hall."

There was no hat in the living room or in the hall. Behind the curtains, Daisy found a very shiny bag of marbles. On the bookshelves she found her favourite book. She out her treasure beside Calliope and the satsuma and chocolate and crisps. She waited patiently to be told the next places she should hunt for the hat.

"I think... you're going to have to try the garden, petal."

Daisy nodded. She told Gran on the way passed the kitchen that she was just going to be in the garden looking for the hat and set off outside. In the garden she found a brand new packet of chalks, sitting on the slabs; a very, very bouncy ball, inside Gran's washing basket under the washing lines; a pocket-sized kaleidoscope, full of beautiful colours; a big snail, two butterfly and a bumble bee, in the flower bed. She took everything inside (except the snail and butterflies and bumble bee, they were very busy) and put everything she'd found together beside her snacks and doll and marbles and book.

"No luck?" Grandad looked very crestfallen.

"I'm sorry," Daisy said. She sat up beside him once again and gave him a big cuddle.

"We might have to get you a new one," Daisy told him gently. She remembered when she lost her favourite glittery hair band at the beach.

"I can't think of anywhere else to try. Ahh, I give up, Daisy. Except," he was looking down at her now with a mischievous grin, "What about... on top of the TV?"

Daisy was about to ask how on Earth his hat that he wore all the time could possibly be missing on top of the TV that he'd been sitting in front of the whole time... but when she turned around, that's exactly where it was. Daisy couldn't believe it,

"How did we miss it all this time?"

"We're rubbish detectives, Daisy. Rubbish." Daisy fetched the hat and tossed it up towards Grandad's head. It landed on his face and he laughed,

"I hope you'll excuse me, darling, but that was very hard work," he winked, "And I need a nap after all that exertion."

"Are you okay, Grandad?" he did look tired.

"Yes. But operations can make you feel sleepy for a while. Nothing to worry about, the more I sleep the faster I'll heal. Probably."

Grandad tipped back his head and lifted his hat down over his eyes. He was quietly snoring very soon. Gran came through and shook her head at Grandad, gently taking the remote out of his hand. Daisy played on the carpet, with all the things she'd found that afternoon. The Sunday roast was cooking in the oven and Mum and Dad would be back soon for dinner. Gran turned on the darts and Daisy played all afternoon while Grandad slept soundly underneath his hat.

Learning to Swim

This is the story of how Mariah learned to swim.

Mariah was at a birthday party with her friends from school. It was Christopher's birthday and they were in a huge soft play centre. Everyone was having lots of fun racing around, hiding from one another and diving into the enormous ball pool.

At lunchtime, Christopher's Mum called out,

"Come on everyone, time to eat!" and all of the children came running from their hiding places to sit around a big table. On top of the table were bowls and dishes and trays of party food.

Mariah was sitting in between Christopher and Lucy, eating little triangle-shaped sandwiches and some slices of cucumber.

"This party is so much fun, Christopher, thanks for inviting me!" Lucy was leaning around Mariah so Christopher could hear her over the noise of children chattering while they ate.

"Yeah," Mariah agreed, "Thanks, this is a great party!"

Christopher smiled a wide smile, clearly pleased everyone was enjoying themselves.

"For *my* birthday," Lucy continued, "I'm going to have a party at the swimming pool. I've already decided."

Mariah immediately began to feel very worried. Lucy and Christopher kept talking but she didn't listen to what they were saying. She looked at her plate and tried not to show how nervous she felt. Mariah couldn't go to a swimming pool party. But Lucy was one of her best friends, how could she not go to her party? She imagined sitting at the side with the grown ups while everyone had fun in the water. No, that would be horrible. She wouldn't be able to go.

It may seem strange that Mariah was so very upset about the idea of her friend's birthday party. But Mariah had a secret, a secret that no one in her class knew about. Mariah couldn't swim.

She was quiet for the rest of the party, hiding in one of the tunnels with spy holes, looking out at everyone and wondering what to do. When Mum came to pick her up, she ran to meet her, glad to be going home. She remembered to say thank you to Christopher's Mum and Dad when she said goodbye but breathed a sigh of relief as they left the soft play building and got to the car.

As Mum buckled her seatbelt, Mariah burst into, rather noisy tears.

"What's wrong, Em?" Mum looked surprisingly calm, considering her daughter was crying loudly in the back seat of the car, "Did you fall out with someone? Or are you just tired? Did you eat too much cake?"

When Mariah didn't stop crying, Mum began to drive. Once they were out of the car park and on the way home, Mariah found it much easier to talk.

"Mum, Lucy says she's having her birthday party at the swimming pool and I can't go because I can't swim but she'll be so upset if I don't go on her birthday when I went on everyone else's birthday and I'd have to sit at the side of the pool with the parents and everyone will find out I can't swim!"

Mum shook her head gently and smiled into the rear-view mirror, so Mariah could see.

"That's not a difficult problem to solve, Em. I'm pretty sure Lucy's birthday isn't for a few months. You're just going to have to learn to swim."

Mariah thought about it. That did seem to be a solution to her problem. But learning to swim was *hard*. She'd tried it before and felt very frightened.

"Will you teach me?" Mariah asked.

"Well, we tried that and it didn't work- I'm not the best teacher. No, it's important now that you learn for real, this time. Let's call Aunty Jess when we get home. That's the answer."

Aunty Jess was Mum's sister, who used to be a lifeguard. She had very, very long hair and always had her fingernails painted. She also had tattoos on her arms, of suns and moons and stars. Mariah liked them, though Mum always told her she was not to think of getting any tattoos. Yes, Aunty Jess was the answer to the problem. Mariah relaxed and stopped worrying about Lucy's birthday party.

Aunty Jess was very enthusiastic about teaching Mariah how to swim. She came over to visit the very next day and demonstrated some swimming techniques in the middle of the living room carpet, and got Mariah to copy her. After a while, she declared she was ready.

"Right, guys, I'll pick Em up from school on Tuesdays and Thursday and we'll go straight to the pool. We'll be home in time for dinner," she turned to Mum, "Remember I'm vegetarian and I hate sweetcorn."

"Well, we'll need to get a swimming costume, we've not been to the-"

Aunty Jess held up her hand, "Already sorted, sis. Check it out."

From her handbag Aunty Jess produced a shiny silver swimming costume with a big, rainbow-coloured flower in the middle of the chest. Mum gasped,

"Where did you find *that?*" she looked horrified.

Mariah loved it. She raced to her room to try it on and didn't want to take it off again. Aunty Jess finished her cup of coffee and got up to go,

"I will see you at 3 o'clock on Tuesday. Be ready," and she winked at Mariah. Mariah winked back.

The first week of lessons did not go particularly well. Aunty Jess didn't drive Mariah to the leisure centre near her school, but a few miles further, to a very old fashioned kind of pool. There were hardly any people there,

"So we don't bump into people we know and end up chatting away instead of getting down to work!" Aunty Jess explained. Mariah thought this was an excellent idea but when she got changed into her special swimming costume and reached the side of the pool, she remembered all the reasons that she hadn't learned to swim before. She was frightened of the water. The pool looked big and deep and scary.

Aunty Jess did some laps up and down the pool to warm up while Mariah watched. It did look fun. She did want to learn to swim. Eventually, she sat down on the steps leading into the pool. Her top half was still completely dry, but her legs were in the water. Aunty Jess swam up and said,

"Perfect! Now we can practise using your legs." And, for the first two lessons, that was all they did. Mariah sat on the steps at the very edge of the big, blue swimming pool and practised using her legs, making the shapes and kicking the way Aunty Jess showed her.

The next week, when she sat on the step, Aunty Jess shook her head.

"We're doing arms this week, darling. You need to stand on the bottom step, so your shoulders are under."

Mariah found this much more frightening but she managed. By the end of the second week she had practised using her legs and her arms in the water, but not together.

On the third week, Aunty Jess told Mariah,

"Today, you swim."

And she did, sort of. Mariah lay her body flat and practised her arms and her legs *at the some time* - while Aunty Jess held her body in both her hands, to keep her afloat. They did this for a few weeks, and every time Aunt Jess suggested removing even one of her hands from underneath Mariah, the poor girl shrieked. So, they practised her arms and legs together for weeks and weeks. Mariah was having lots of fun with Aunty Jess, but she didn't think she'd ever be able to swim without someone holding her up in the water.

One day, Aunty Jess said,

"We're having dinner at a cafe near here tonight. To celebrate all your hard work!"

The cafe was lovely. The tables and chairs were made of dark, twisty wood. The ceiling was covered in hanging plants and the walls were covered in sparkly fairy lights. All of the paintings on the walls were of fruits and vegetables.

"This is my favourite place to eat," Aunty Jess explained, "It's vegetarian, but I'm sure we'll find something you'll like." Mariah felt like a celebrity; all of the staff seemed to know Aunty Jess and they all asked Mariah her name and smiled at her.

They ordered two veggie burgers and chips. Mariah chomped happily at her food; she was always hungry after spending time in the swimming pool. Aunty Jess pointed one of her chips at her.

"You're making brilliant progress, Em. I think you might be a natural."

Mariah chewed a big bite of veggie burger. It was delicious. She swallowed and answered,

"I don't think I am. I'm too scared to do it by myself."

"Well," Aunty Jess answered, "That's exactly how I felt! Until I realised that... you promise not to tell anyone?"

Mariah had no idea what Aunty Jess was about to tell her, but she wanted to know. She nodded.

Aunty Jess whispered her secret, "I'm... well, at least, I *think* I might be... part mermaid!"

Mariah didn't reply. She didn't know what to say.

"And, if I am then... well. There's a chance you might be, too."

Mariah listened, not quite sure if she believed her, as Aunty Jess told stories about her great great great great great great great great great grandmother, the mermaid.

That night, Mariah dreamed of swimming in a beautiful blue ocean. She *had* to learn to swim.

In the morning on the next day she was going swimming, her Mum reminded her to put her swimming kit in her school bag.

"How are you two getting on? You'll nearly be there by now I'm sure. Anyway, Lucy's party is in three weeks- her Mum called me last night and mentioned it."

Mariah put down her spoon- she suddenly couldn't eat any more cereal. Three weeks? She'd never be ready in time. She was miserable all day at school, dreading going swimming. She stayed quiet when Aunty Jess picked her up. But, once they got into the pool, Mariah started to feel a bit better.

"I was wondering when you were going to give me a smile! See, you must be part mermaid, like I said. You're happy when you're in the water."

When Aunty Jess held Mariah up in the water, she remembered all the things she'd be taught; what to do with her arms and legs, to keep her breathing steady. But, this time, when she closed her eyes, she imagined the beautiful blue ocean once again.

In her imagination she swam through the clear, warm water, watching schools of fish swim in perfect harmony together through the water. She could see brightly coloured seaweed and pretty, shining crabs scuttling along the sea bed. She imagined swimming alongside a sleek dolphin. She felt calm and happy and relaxed. When she raised her head to take a breath, suddenly she became aware that she was moving through the swimming pool, not the sea, and there was no dolphin by her side- it was

Aunty Jess! And she was swimming beside Mariah-and Mariah was swimming, too! All on her own with no help at all. She reached the other side of the pool and grabbed the edge to let herself float. She didn't feel frightened of the water now. Aunty Jess smiled her huge smile and said, "Let's try that again, Mariah the mermaid."

For the last two weeks before the party, Mariah tried very hard in the swimming pool. She wanted to be able to swim as confidently as she could. Everyone at school was talking about the party the day before and Mariah felt her nerves growing once again, despite all the hours of practise she'd had. What if she got there and forgot? What if that fear came back and she couldn't do it?

When she was getting ready for the party the next morning, her Mum said,

"Oh! Almost forgot. Aunty Jess gave me these, they're for you to wear today. Do you like them?"

Mum was holding out two shining iridescent silver hair clips. In the shape of seashells. They were beautiful- and just like something a mermaid might wear.

At the pool, all of her friends raced from the changing rooms to get into the water. They were all splashing and having fun. She stood watching them for a moment. Lucy's Mum said,

"You okay, Mariah? Your swimming costume is amazing, very cool. And I like those hair clips. You're definitely dressed for a party!"

Mariah smiled and touched her hair clips and remembered the ocean and the fish and the dolphin. She could do it. Before she got in the pool, she turned to Lucy's Mum and asked,

"What are those things Lucy is wearing?"

"Ah. They are armbands. You fill them up with air and they float, to keep you on top of the water. Lucy's not quite got the hang of swimming on her own yet. She was a bit worried about the party, but she just loves the water. Look, Robin and Tim have armbands, too. I think that made her feel better."

Lucy's Mum winked at Mariah. Mariah was so happy that she laughed. She had been so worried, and now she was one of the best swimmers here! She had never been so excited to get into the pool and she splashed around with her friends all afternoon.

The Useless Tree

Darius lived in a big, old house with his Mum and Dad, his aunty, uncle and cousins and both of his Mum's parents. His cousins were a little younger than him but they were fun to play games with outside. Darius would chase them and they would shriek and giggle with excitement.

Their favourite place to run and chase one another was amongst the trees at the bottom of the garden. It was a tiny orchard; each tree grew different fruit; oranges, cherries, lemons, apples, pears.They would run amongst them together until they were exhausted and collapse onto the soft grass beneath the little trees, sheltering from the hot sun in the shade of their leaves. There was one tree, however, that didn't grow any fruit.

Darius remembered that when his Grandad used to pick fruit from the trees in the summer, he would always give the fruitless tree a little kick on his way past. He would mutter, "Useless tree," or "Pointless thing," or "What a waste of space!" as he went to collect fruit from the trees that grew delicious things to eat. Darius' grandad was too old to pick the fruit himself and now his mother did it. She didn't kick the fruitless tree, or say anything to it as she walked b. She simply completely ignored it. Some Springs, the tree would grow pale orange-red blossoms. On those years, Darius would say, "This might be the year the tree gives fruit!" but his Mum would smile and say nothing and his Grandad would shake his fist towards the garden.

As Darius got older, he began to run around the trees less and less. He enjoyed reading and drawing and painting and he liked to be in the sunshine, so he still spent a lot of time in the little orchard at the end of the garden. Although his Grandad and his Mum thought the fruitless tree was useless, it was Darius' favourite tree in the orchard. There was a branch that he could reach if he jumped up and grabbed with his hands and he often swung himself up into the tree to read books. It wasn't very high up, but the leaves shielded him from the sun, as well as from any parents or uncles who might have chores in mind for him.

He drew and painted the garden often and he always painted the fruitless tree right in the middle, with the others crowded behind. He would stroke its trunk and talk to it, sometimes, saying it was the tree he loved the best. He visited the tree almost every day, wrapping himself up warmly to sit in its branches to read, even after summer had turned to autumn. When winter came and all the leaves fell from the trees, he still painted the garden, with his favourite tree in the middle, from his bedroom window.

The following spring, all of the trees in the orchard blossomed- including the fruitless tree. This had happened before, but these were big, beautiful blooms, this time. Darius thought the colour looked a lot like his aunty's red nail varnish- bold and bright. This year, however, he didn't tell anyone he thought the tree might bear fruit. He pretended not to notice but, as soon as it was warm enough, he was back in the tree once again. Sometimes, he read out loud from the book he brought to the tree. He always said thank you to the tree before he climbed down, resting his forehead against the bark and feeling peaceful and safe.

He was in the garden with his Grandad, drinking lemonade and playing cards, one bright afternoon when a neighbour called out to them, over the hedge,

"Is that useless tree going to show us something new this year, huh?"

Grandad shook his head and waved his walking stick at the woman who laughed and laughed. Darius chose to stay quiet. That tree had been in the garden for a long time, since before his grandfather was born. It would be pretty miraculous if it grew fruit now.

One day, Darius' mother was calling him from the house. He was inside the tree, daydreaming and well hidden from her. He stayed where he was and ignored her calling to him. After a few minutes, his Mum appeared at the foot of the tree. Darius almost fell off his branch!

"I know you can hear me, Darius. And I know you hide in this tree and I will tell everyone else about your hiding place if you don't get down here now and help-"

His mother was staring at Darius with a look of shock on her face. Darius raised his hand to his head, thinking he must have a nose bleed, she was looking at him with such fright. Silently she raised her hand and pointed upwards, to something just above his head. Darius looked up and he smiled. He didn't feel shocked.

"Darius… it's. *Fruit*. In the useless tree!"

They decided to keep the fruit a secret, until it grew and ripened and could be picked. Darius' grandad didn't walk amongst the trees in the summer anymore; he was old and it was too hot. Darius' aunt and uncle and dad all noticed but they kept the secret, too. The fruits grew very large and pale pink. They didn't look like anything else on the trees in the small orchard. When Darius and his mum picked them together, she told him what they were,

"Pomegranates. The fruit of love. Funny, coming from a tree no one loves."

Darius knew that it wasn't true; the tree *was* loved. But he simply nodded as he helped his mum gather the fruit so they could surprise his Grandad. Darius looked forward to it almost as much as he looked forward to tasting his first ever pomegranate.

Hallowe'en

Rachael ran home from school. She was very excited. Today was Hallowe'en and this year, for the first time ever, her Mum said she'd let Rachael go out with her friends on her own! Lisa and Amanda were going to stay at Rachael's for a sleepover, after they'd got lots of sweets.

Usually, Rachael had to go out on Hallowe'en with her Mum and her little brother, Liam, while her friends went without her. Mum had finally agreed that Rachael didn't have to go with her and Liam. It was a very safe place on Hallowe'en, where they lived. They knew almost all their neighbours and everyone was kind and friendly.

Hallowe'en was great fun where they lived. Most people decorated their houses and gave out lots of sweets to visitors. It was Rachael's favourite night of the year; she loved getting dressed up and going out in the dark. She loved seeing everyone in their costumes and trying to guess who was hiding under their wig or hat or make up. She loved the warm smell as dripping candles glowed inside carved pumpkins, heating up their insides and giving off their scent. She loved going home with a bag heavy with sweets, some of her favourites as well as things she'd never tried before.

163

When she got home, Rachael immediately went to her room to begin getting ready. Her friends weren't coming until six o-clock but she wanted her costume to be perfect. Her Mum was in the shower, which was a bit unusual, but Rachael sat down to paint her nails with black nail varnish. She was going to dress up as a vampire this year.

Just as she was finishing the very last nail, her Mum appeared at her bedroom door. She was all wrapped up in her dressing gown.

"Hey, darling. How was school?"

"Great!" Rachael was in a very good mood.

"I'm really sorry, Rach, but-"

Rachael froze. Her Mum had promised she could go out with her friends this year. Had she changed her mind?

"What is it?" Rachael's face was so horrified that her Mum came and sat down beside her on the bed.

"I can't go anywhere tonight. I was sent home from work this morning and I've been asleep all day. I feel terrible!"

Rachael said, "Okay, but I can still-"

Her Mum interrupted, "You need to take Liam with you. You can't leave him behind."

"No! He's too immature, he'll ruin it!"

Her Mum sighed, "Rachael, can you imagine if you couldn't go out on Hallowe'en when you were his age? He'll be heartbroken."

Rachael knew her Mum was right. Liam loved Hallowe'en, too. She nodded her head, wondering what she was going to tell her friends. Then she asked,

"What about the sleepover?"

"Sorry Rachael. I'm really feeling ill. Your nails look really cool, by the way. Suits you."

Once Mum was gone, Rachael flopped down on the bed, waiting for her nails to try before she got changed into her costume. Her excitement for the night had almost completely disappeared.

Lisa and Amanda both shouted *BOO* when Rachael opened the front door at six o'clock.

"Bad news… Mum isn't well. We need to take Liam with us."

Lisa laughed, "That's okay! It'll still be really fun. Liam's sweet. You look really good, by the way. What's he dressed as?"

"I don't actually know... you guys look great, too!" Lisa was dressed as Dorothy from the Wizard of Oz which was her favourite film. She had sparkly ruby slippers and everything. Amanda was dressed as a zombie. Her Mum was a make-up artist and she looked really frightening. It was already dark and Rachael was itching to get going. She called up stairs, "Come *on*, Liam, are you coming or what?!"

Her Mum appeared at the top of the stairs,
"Wow, you three look brilliant! Rach, don't shout, please. I feel terrible."

The girls all made sympathetic faces, until Liam burst out of his bedroom. Lisa laughed, Amanda said, "Aww!" and Rachael said, "He's not wearing *that?*"

Her Mum held Liam's hand to help him walk down the stairs. He had lots of branches and twigs all over a black pair of trousers and a black top. Some even had leaves clinging to them. He was extremely proud of his costume,

"Rach, Liam's been saying he wanted to dress up as a tree since *last* Hallowe'en. We;ve been making this all of last week, did you really not notice?"

Rachel was not happy. Not only did she have to take her brother with her the very first time she went out on her own at Hallowe'en, he was dressed as a tree! She hoped no one from school saw them but she realised there was nothing she could do,

"Right!" she said, "Let's get going!" Mum took some pictures of them all before they left. Rachael looked like a very moody vampire indeed.

They knocked on doors together, Rachael looking moody and serious, Amanda looking really scary and Lisa smiling sweetly and clicking her red slippers together, which made everyone laugh. Liam was a bit shy, and clung on to Rachael's cloak as people asked him about his costume. As they were walking to the next street, Lisa said,

"I want to bring Liam with me every year; you definitely get more sweets if you've got a little kid with you." She turned around to high five Liam, who was delighted.

"Yeah," Amanda agreed. She was already eating a piece of toffee as they walked.

"Maybe. As long as he sorts out a better costume." Liam stopped walking, "Do you not like my costume?"

Rachael kept walking, not wanting to stop, "It's just... weird, that's all. It's Hallowe'en. You're supposed to be *scary*. Or dress up to look like someone. Not just stick stuff all over yourself and say you're a-"

Rachael turned around but Liam was gone. She whirled in frantic circles. How could he have just disappeared? She felt her heart hammering inside her chest. She was supposed to be looking after him and he'd be so scared and alone…

Lisa and Amanda realised what was going on. They called, "Liam! Liam?"

It wasn't until Rachael called out, "Liam, where are you?!" that they heard a reply.

"I'm over here, look!"

Liam was standing not very far from Rachael. He was at the very edge of a garden, beside a tree. He was very well camouflaged in his costume. He ran over to Rachael who knelt down to cuddle him.

"Liam! I'm sorry. Your costume *is* good, okay? It's the best one I've seen tonight."

"And it did make you scared!"

All three of the girls laughed and laughed as Liam smiled up at the triumphantly,

"Yes Liam," his sister agreed, "That is the most scared anyone's costume has ever made me feel!"

They got home that night with more sweets than ever before. Everyone loved Liam's tree costume and thought the girls were so kind for taking him out with them. When they got home, Mum was fast asleep in bed. Amanda and Lisa had brought sleeping bags and Rachael scooped up her duvet and Liam's and they all went to the living room. They washed off their makeup and changed into pyjamas. They piled pillows on the floor and lay down there for the night. They whispered ghost stories to one another, very careful not to frighten Liam too much. When he fell asleep, they told scarier and scarier stories until they fell asleep.

In the morning, Mum came through to find them all asleep on the living room floor, with Liam in the middle,

"Everyone okay?!"

"Mum!" said Rachael, "We weren't back too late, I promise, but you were asleep so we all just came in here so we wouldn't wake you up!"

"Thank you. I feel much better this morning. Did you have fun, darling?" she asked Liam.

"Mum," he said, "I had the scariest costume and we got the most sweets of anyone and I'm going to ask the girls if next year we can be the ghostbusters.

"Wow, sounds like you had a great time!" Mum winked and whispered, *thank you* to the girls.

"Now... who would like pancakes for breakfast?" Liam cheered and Mum set off to the kitchen.

"I've never seen ghostbusters," said Amanda.

"Me either. It's his favourite," Rachael answered.

"Well," said Lisa as she rolled up the sleeping bags, "Sounds like we're all going to have to watch it."

Uncle David's Dilemma

Noelle and Nathan visited their Uncle David every week. Uncle David was their dad's brother and lived very close to their school. They would walk to visit him after school on a Friday, as Mum and Dad were both at work that day.

Uncle David worked from home. The twins knew he was a kind of scientist who wrote lots of long papers and books about science. He often went to visit universities and hospitals to teach people about what he knew. He was a very clever man and he always taught them interesting things about the world. He showed them interesting films about plants and animals; he was teaching them both to play chess (well, he was trying his best); he showed them how to write code on a computer.

Uncle David lived with Aunt Olivia. Aunt Olivia worked from home a lot, too; she was an artist. But for two days a week, she taught art classes in the nearby college. Once of the days she taught each week was a Friday, when Noelle and Nathan visied. She was always very tired- Friday was a long, long day for her. One Friday, she burned her hand while she was boiling pasta and chopping up mushrooms. She sat down, very upset. Noelle rushed to get a cold, damp cloth for the burn and Nathan asked if she was alright. They'd been sitting at the kitchen table with Uncle David and the chess board as she cooked.

"David, I'm sorry, but I have to ask you. *Please* will you do the cooking on a Friday night? Just one day a week. It stresses me out having to feed you all after working all day," she turned to the twins and said, "Sorry for getting upset, guys."

But the twins both thought she was quite right to be upset. Now that they thought about it, it did seem unfair that she was cooking dinner for everyone after teaching all day. Uncle David wrapped his arms around her and kissed her cheek.

"Why don't we make Friday takeaway night?" he asked sweetly. Aunt Olivia was not happy.

"*No*, David. We have a takeaway on a Saturday night. I don't want takeaway on a Friday. I want you to make something for me."

Uncle David promised he would make the dinner on a Friday in the future. Noelle put the chess board away quietly while Nathan set the table for dinner. Uncle David watched Aunt Olivia as she finished making the pasta and mushroom sauce.

The next Friday, Noelle and Nathan let themselves in to Uncle David's house and were very surprised to see that he wasn't at the computer in the living room. The headed to the kitchen table to do their homework. Uncle David was standing up on a chair, reaching far into a high up cupboard. He jumped when the twins said hello, startled. Then he gave them a weak smile as he came down from the chair and said, "Hello, you two."

"Uncle David, what's wrong with you?" asked Noelle.

"Yeah," said Nathan, "You look all worried."

"Guys. This is really embarrassing, but… Well, Liv wants me to cook dinner for the four of us tonight and… I don't know how to cook!"

"At all?" the twins said, at the same time.

"At all," he answered, "I kept meaning to study a bit during the week but… I forgot. I've been really busy."

They all sat down at the table.

"Okay," said Noelle, "What would you like to make?"
"Oh… I don't know!"

"Relax," Nathan said, "We'll help you. Let's start with something simple."

"Spaghetti? I know we had pasta last week, but maybe…?"

The twins nodded, "We know how to make tomato sauce for spaghetti," Nathan told his Uncle, "We just need two tins of tomatoes and onion and garlic. That's it." Noelle spotted half a bottle of wine by the cooker and she pointed at it, "Dad says if you splash some wine in it makes it even better."

The twins went to the shop for the tomatoes while Uncle David got the rest of the ingredients ready. They showed him how to sautee the onions and garlic and added the tomatoes and wine,

"Dad says *just let that cook away for a while*, so I think we just leave it like that," Noelle said. Uncle David nodded, "That sounds right."

When Aunt Olivia came home, Uncle David was just putting out dinner on the table. He'd boiled the spaghetti while the twins did their homework.

"Mmmmm," said Aunt Olivia, "Thanks David."

"The pasta's... ehh... a bit, crunchy. In some places," Uncle David said.

"Sorry," Nathan added, "That part was our job."

"Well this is a great try," Aunt Olivia said. The sauce was delicious and everyone ate all the spaghetti that wasn't still a little raw.

The next week, Uncle David was a little bit more prepared.

"Okay," he said, "We're going to make baked potatoes this week. That way, we just have to heat up some beans to go with them. Can't undercook *those*." He looked very pleased with himself.

He had four big potatoes waiting on the kitchen table.

"So. What do we do now?" he asked.

Noelle sighed, "First, we need to turn on the oven so it can heat up. Mum pokes holes all over the potatoes and puts a little bit of oil on each of them. Then they go in the oven."

"For how long?" Uncle David asked.

Both twins shrugged, "Ages," said Nathan.

Uncle David put the potatoes in the oven and set the timer for two hours. He did some work on his computer while the twins did their homework. He was reading a book to Noelle and Nathan when Aunt Olivia came in.

"I think dinner might be ready, guys...?" she called. Uncle David ran to the oven and opened it. A big waft of dark smoke came out and rolled towards the ceiling.

"Oops," said Noelle, "I was meant to be keeping an eye on the time for them! Sorry."

"It's okay," said Olivia, "It's just the bottoms that are a bit black. I'm sure they'll be delicious."

She had a shower while the twins set the table and Uncle David heated the beans.

"Delicious!" Aunt Olivia declared. There were definitely no raw parts that week.

The next Friday, Uncle David had a huge bag from the shop. He took out vegetables and washed them,

"Salad!" he announced, "I can't burn that *or* serve it raw!"

Once he had washed everything, the twins helped him chop. There were a lot of vegetables for the salad. Lettuce, cucumber, spring onions, yellow peppers, carrots, tomatoes, radishes and avocado. They chopped everything up neatly and threw it into the bowl.

"Uncle David, you're bleeding!" Noelle said.

Nathan ran off to get the plasters from the first aid kit to cover the cut.

"You need to practise your knife skills," he told his uncle.

Everyone had a big helping of salad for dinner that night; Aunt Olivia drizzled olive oil and vinegar all over and it was really delicious.

The next Friday, Nathan and Noelle were shocked to find Uncle David cooking in the kitchen when they came in from school.

"What are you doing?" said Nathan.

"Oh, you haven't cut yourself, have you?" asked Noelle.

Uncle David laughed, "Relax, you two. I'm making pizza. Come and see."

He was rolling out the dough on the counter, making a big, wonky circle.

"I remembered that I used to make bread with my Dad when I was about your age. Pizza dough is very similar. And I've made the sauce for the base, I made it the same way you showed me." He was smiling and his t-shirt was covered in flour. The twins were still a bit suspicious,

"What about toppings?" said Noelle.

"Yeah, what goes on the top?" Nathan asked.

"Guys. I have *eaten* pizza before. Look, there's going to be two. You can share one, they're pretty big. Everything for the top gets chopped up, just like when we made salad. You can choose what you want."

Uncle David had the toppings waiting on the kitchen table. There was mozzarella cheese, olives, mushrooms, jalapeno chilli peppers, tomatoes.

"Everything, please!" the twins said together.

"Hmm… even jalapenos?" Uncle David asked.

"Yeah," said Noelle, "we usually cut them into smaller pieces so they're not *too* hot."

"Great idea. You two do your homework and then set the table. They don't take long in the oven, so we'll put them in once Liv's home."

Aunt Olivia was *very* pleasantly surprised when she came home. The pizzas went into the oven to cook and nothing was too burnt or too raw. No one was cut, although Uncle David was still covered in flour. When he went to change his t-shirt, she sat beside the twins,

"Thank you so much," she told them, "Pizza is my favourite!"

They looked at each other, "We didn't help. Not this time… honestly" said Nathan.

Aunt Olivia was impressed, "Really? Not one bit?"

"No!" said Noelle, "We did before, when he kept getting everything wrong, but he seems to… be really good at making pizza!"

Aunt Olivia gave them both a hug, "Thank you for helping him. He's so clever but he sometimes… gets nervous about doing new things. I'm so glad you two are here to keep an eye on him."

Uncle David came back into the kitchen just as the timer went off to let them know the pizza was ready to come out of the oven. From that day on, Friday was pizza day. Aunt Olivia could come home after work and relax and the twins no longer had to worry about Uncle David hurting himself or setting something on fire.

Freya & the Imps in the Oak Tree

Freya woke up one morning to hear an almighty racket! She looked out of her window and saw diggers and drills and lots of people wearing yellow hard hats. *Builders,* she thought to herself. They were working behind a tall silver fence, to keep people out of their way. Freya sighed. It was close to where she liked to play, in the big green field beside her house. She'd have to stay inside the garden now, but it would probably still be quite noisy.

At breakfast, she asked her Dad what was going on. "Building houses," he said. He didn't sound happy about it, "Probably all over the field. We're going to have to put up with that noise for a while, I should think." He sighed and read the newspaper. Freya thought about it and decided she didn't mind too much. Maybe there would be more children to play with, if they got more neighbours. The ones who lived here now were a bit older than Freya, and she would have liked to have some friends. After breakfast, Freya went out to play in the garden. In her pocket she had a handful of raisins. She ducked underneath the hedge between her garden and the field and round the base of the huge oak tree. She sat down and, when she was sure no one was watching her, she took the raisins out of her pocket and put them gently on top of one of the oak tree's roots.

A moment later, two tiny faces looked out from a hole in the bottom of the tree. Once they recognised Freya, the two tiny imps leapt out from their hiding place to say hello and grab the raisins. The imps were smaller than Freya's hand.

"Hello Ilona, hello, Ivan," she said very, very softly.

"How are you Freya! What's that terrible noise! It woke me up this morning!"

"Ahh, it woke me up too. And it may go on a little longer, I'm afraid. Dad says that the builders over there are building houses. I think that takes quite a bit of time, building a house."

"Fiddlesticks," said Ivan, "More houses means more people."

Ilona looked worried as she added, "And more people means more chances of someone finding us."

"You know what'll happen then," said Ivan.

"I know, I know, don't w-"

Ilona interrupted her, "We'll be captured and kept in a cage for people to look at us! We"l be trapped forever! We'll be-"

"Stop!" It was Freya's turn to interrupt this time, "Stay calm. I will not let that happen. I know this is the best tree for miles around, but if you are in any danger, I will help you move somewhere safe. I promise."

Ivan took a big bite of the grape, hardly making a dent in it as his mouth was so small, "I love these. Thanks, Freya." Freya smiled. Sometimes it was stressful keeping the secret of two imps living in an oak tree beside her house, but Freya knew she would never tell anyone. She didn't want to upset them, but she knew the imps were right. If people knew about them, they might kidnap them and take them somewhere else. They weren't doing anyone any harm and they were good company for Freya.
"Look, it's very noisy, but they're still quite a bit away from here. The houses might not come that close at all. We just need to stay alert."

Unfortunately, a few days later, a letter came to the house that ruined Freya's hopes of protecting the imps. Her dad read it to her over breakfast. It was from the Council. They were going to cut down the oak tree, as it's huge roots were interfering with the digging work. Dad shook his head and Freya quietly began to cry.

"Oh love, I know how special that tree is to you. I'm so sorry. It says here it's going ahead, I don't think there's anything we can do."

"Do?" asked Freya.

"Well, you know, sometimes when there's a plan people don't like they do something about it. Like protest. But I don't think they'll listen to us now. They're cutting it down next week."

Dad dried Freya's tears with a sleeve of her dressing gown before he went upstairs for a shower. He'd left his phone on the table. Freya picked it up and opened the back door, so her dad wouldn't hear her. She pressed the magnifying glass button, the one that meant search. And then she said, "protest trees" quietly into the phone.

It made a *bleep* sound, and then lots and lots of words came up. Freya looked until she found pictures. There were lots of pictures of people with trees. Some of them were holding signs, some of them were holding hands in a circle around the tree. Some of them had climbed into the tree. None of these were any good. She couldn't write very well, yet, and it was just her. No one else. Then she saw a picture that gave her an idea. Before Dad got out of the shower, she got a ball of wool from the cupboard and ran to her tree. The imps were asking what on earth she was doing, but she didn't have time to explain. She ran round and round the tree with the ball of wool. When it was nearly finished, she sat beside Ivan and Ilona's front door, and tied the wool around her waist, looping it around a few times like she'd done to the tree. The poor imps were very worried about the way Freya was acting.

Once she was all tied up, she leaned back against the tree to quietly explain,

"It's protest. The Council wants to cut down this tree to build the houses," Ilona and Ivan grabbed one another, "But I'm not going to let them. I'm going to stay here until they give up."

Freya was as good as her word. She stayed tied to the tree for the whole week. Her dad brought her food and water and, when everyone was in bed and no one could see, Freya would sneak inside to go to the toilet. After two days, one of the men from the building site came over,

"You're really sweet, little girl," he said with a sad smile, "But it won't work. They're building these houses. That tree is coming down."

Freya didn't reply. She just stayed where she was. She was *not* going to move. The next day, her dad was rubbing sunscreen on her nose when two people came over. One had a notebook and the other held a camera.

"Hello, excuse me? Are you- well, of course you are, you're the only little girl tied to a tree around here. So, you're the protestor? Can we ask why you want to save this particular tree?"

Freya started to panic. Were people going to discover her imp friends because of her protest? She'd been trying to save them but now she was the one putting them in danger!

"She won't answer you," her dad said, "She's taken a vow of silence," he turned to Freya and winked.

"She's protesting the plans to cut down this majestic oak tree. It's very special to her."

The one with the camera asked, "Can we...?" and Freya's dad nodded. He took lots of pictures of her, while the woman with the notebook scribbled down everything she said. They left shortly afterwards and her Dad said,

"I hope you're ready Freya. There will be plenty of that for the next few days. Everyone is going to want to interview you. Just refuse to speak. Let your actions speak for you. I'm very proud of you," he kissed her on the forehead.

He was right. There were lots more reporters and photographers. There were TV cameras, too. And, even more baffling to Freya, there were more protestors, too. None of them tied themselves up but they carried signs and sat around the tree during the day. They all went home at night time, but they came back in the morning! Freya hardly had any time to speak to Ivan and Ilona. She didn't know what she would do if they did cut the tree down. How would she smuggle the imps away and help them escape? She needed her protest to work. She slept with her fingers crossed.

When the day came for the tree to be cut down, there were lots and lots of people there. Many of them tried to talk to Freya but her dad stood beside her and held her hand and she shook her head when they asked if she would speak. Her dad had been right. There was nothing she could say that would be better than tying herself to the tree.

There were TV cameras, photographers, reporters, people from the streets all around. Lots of them had gone past the border made by the reporters and sat beside Freya. They chanted, *Save this tree, save this tree!* Freya tried to look brave but she felt really scared as the men arrived to cut down the tree. Were they going to chop her up with that chainsaw when they cut into the tree? A man with a megaphone spoke so everyone in the crowd could hear:

"We have informed you all of our plan to remove this tree as it poses a danger to the foundations of the new homes we are building. Please move away from the area and allow us to safely do our job. If you don't move away, we will have no other choice but to call the police and have you all removed."

The police? Freya felt sick. Was she going to be arrested? But then, she probably wouldn't even care if she was arrested, if Ivan and Ilona were crushed to death under the fallen tree. She felt like she was going to cry. Her dad placed his hand on her shoulder and she knew, even though he was proud of her, that he was going to tell her to give up. She hadn't saved her friends and she couldn't even tell anyone about them.

Just as Freya was about to collapse in a miserable heap, a woman walked past Freya. She had a purple jacket and long dark hair and a beautiful necklace that looked like an acorn. The woman stepped out, right in front of the man with the megaphone. She held something up in her hand, for everyone to see, and called out in a loud voice. She was obviously used to being heard in large crowds.

"Removing this tree is unlawful. There are bats roosting nearby who use this tree as a source of food. All bats are protected in this country, which means you cannot jeopardise their lives by cutting down this tree."

The men were murmuring to themselves. The man with the megaphone spoke quietly, just to the woman.

"I thought they checked all the wildlife stuff? Are you sure?"

"I'm sure they *said* they checked it. I'm quite sure. You can't cut down this tree until you review the wildlife nearby and you'll see that I'm right."

The man spoke into the megaphone, "We will not be removing this tree today after some, err, something important has been brought to our attention. We will contact you all if there is a revised date for the removal of this tree."

Everyone cheered. Dad went into the kitchen and got out a pair of scissors to cut Freya free. She was very happy. Lots of people took photographs of her with the tree and she was smiling in all of them. It was very late when they all finally left.

The next day, she went back to the tree to visit her friends,

"We've got something for you. Something we made." Ilona told her.

Ivan was very excited, "It's a very special thing, that we imps only give to very *very* special people." He ran inside to fetch the special thing.

"And you are an extremely special person, Freya. You saved our home."

Ivan brought out an acorn bigger than he was. He was huffing and puffing a bit under the weight, so she picked it up.

"It's dried and polished, just for you," Ilona explained. It was beautiful.

"Should last forever!" called Ivan.

Freya tied it around her neck with a piece of the wool she'd been tied to the tree with.

"Ahh, that's a good idea, it's lovely as a necklace. It suits you." Ilona said.

Freya wondered where she got the idea from... then she remembered, the woman with the paper, the one who'd stopped the tree being cut down,

"I think that woman, the one who said about the bats, was wearing one the same."

The imps looked at each other with raised eyebrows.

"She must know some imps who think she's very special, too."

Freya decided that she'd try to find the woman again, to thank her for all her help and to ask about her necklace. But, not today. She'd had quite enough excitement to last her a little while.